DEAD IN THE WATER

DEAD IN THE WATER

Ted Wood

CHARLES SCRIBNER'S SONS · NEW YORK

For my father, good man,
good copper.

———————•———————

Library of Congress Cataloging in Publication Data

Wood, Ted.
  Dead in the water.

  I. Title.
PR9199.3.W57D4   1983   813'.54   83–8997
ISBN 0–684–17958–X

1 3 5 7 9 11 13 15 17 19   F/C   20 18 16 14 12 10 8 6 4 2

Printed in the United States of America.

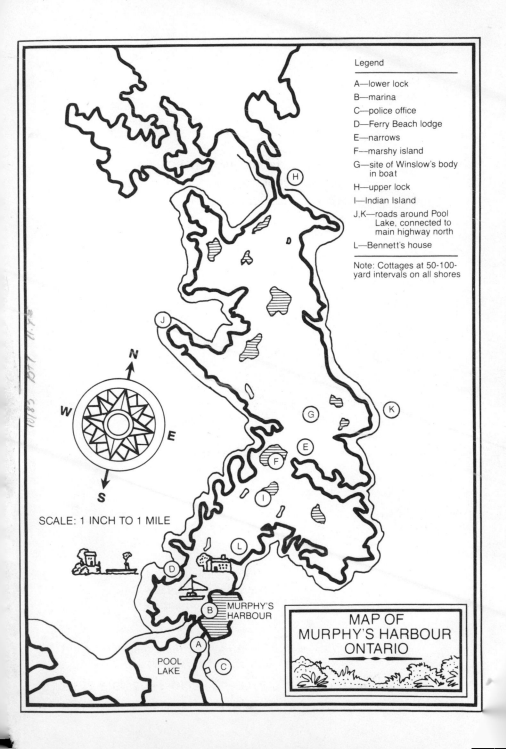

Legend

A—lower lock
B—marina
C—police office
D—Ferry Beach lodge
E—narrows
F—marshy island
G—site of Winslow's body
 in boat
H—upper lock
I—Indian Island
J,K—roads around Pool
 Lake, connected to
 main highway north
L—Bennett's house

Note: Cottages at 50-100-
yard intervals on all shores

SCALE: 1 INCH TO 1 MILE

MURPHY'S
HARBOUR

POOL
LAKE

MAP OF
MURPHY'S HARBOUR
ONTARIO

Three of them were working on the girl. The biggest was
zipping his fly and laughing while the other two took over, trying for the two-at-once trick.

I was off duty. My gun was locked in the safe at the station
and I'd changed into plain clothes, so they didn't even know I
was a policeman. It wouldn't have mattered to the big one,
anyway. He went six four, maybe two eighty. He figured he
was Superman. Until I stuck two fingers into his throat.

It could have ended there, with one dead, if the second one
hadn't come at me. I pinned him but the third one didn't take
the hint and so I had to break the arm on the one I was
holding and put the third one down. He had a knife so I hurt
him.

They arrested me. My own buddies from 52 Division. They
apologized. "It's for your own protection. If we don't, the
papers can tear you to shreds. This way they have to keep
quiet."

That was Inspector Anderson, Superintendent Anderson
now. "It's for your own good," he told me again when I didn't
answer. "You'll be out on bail in an hour and you'll be acquit-

1

ted. You have to understand, nobody likes a policeman who can kill people."

He was right. I was acquitted, after the defense explained that I had been a Canadian volunteer in Viet Nam and had been taught a lot of tricks you don't learn at the police academy in Aylmer, Ontario.

But the morning after, the media took it up and the phone calls started. Then the garbage against the door of the house. I couldn't understand at first what made the public take sides with a bunch of bikies working on a gang rape. But I worked it out as the days passed. It was me they resented. I'd broken faith with the liberals who were slamming me now. When I'd volunteered for service in the States, gone to a war their own guys were running to Canada to avoid, I'd put myself on the other side of some fence. If I'd stayed in northern Ontario and rotted my lungs out in the smelter at the nickel mine, they would have treated me like a brother. Only I didn't, I chose violence, and now it was destroying me.

My wife took it for a week. I took it for three, going out every morning to see what new filth had been written on my car in spray paint, listening to the sneers of the drunks in my patrol area.

And then I gave them their badge back, and their gun, and looked for a different kind of work. Only it's not easy to place yourself when your only real skill is putting people down so they stay down. And that's why I ended up here, in Murphy's Harbour, a resort town just within range of the weekend commuters from Toronto. Nothing violent happens here.

1

I let go of Linda and grabbed the phone. "Chief of Police."

"Still wide awake, eh?" Murphy gave his dry, old-man's chuckle. "Good, won't take you long to get dressed and down the station."

"Okay, Murph. What happened that you have to call me at . . ." I checked the alarm clock. "At three A.M."

"Young Sullivan, Ken Sullivan's kid got himself cut up." I struggled upright. Linda was lying on my left arm. I pried it free. Ken Sullivan was a town councillor. Like it or not, I had to take notice.

"Knife cuts, or what?"

Murphy coughed once, a signal that things were not as bad as they sounded. "No. Outboard propeller. He hit something up by Indian Island, fell out of the boat, and the motor ran over him."

I swore softly and patted Linda's bare shoulder. Murphy went on in his infuriatingly slow, up-country way. "So the girl with him pulled him in."

Now it made sense. Murphy wanted me to talk to the girl.

Other stuff he handled, out of the little Mickey Mouse switch-board in his house over on the point north of the Harbour. But this was an investigation. I could see his eyebrows raise in disgust at the word. It called for the police chief—the whole force in fact—of Murphy's Harbour to turn out of a warm and appealing bed to soothe the feathers of some flustered cottager.

"Couldn't this have waited until tomorrow?"

"It already is tomorrow." He sounded reasonable.

"Okay, so tell her to wait at the police station."

"She's there now," he said, and beat me to the hang-up by a microsecond.

I turned back to Linda, warm, Chanel-scented, every-Friday-come-rain-or-shine Linda. "Where were we?" She showed me and very soon I was up and getting dressed. She watched as I buttoned the pants and tucked in the shirt.

"What a lousy thing to happen on a Friday night." I nodded, concentrating on buckling the Sam Browne with the handcuffs pouch and the .38 Colt Police Special. She sat up, dangling her head to one side. She was a brown-eyed blonde, slim and pale from too much book work. She worked north of Murphy's Harbour and came through every Friday, stopping by like a swallow on her way south. Where she went before or after she never told me. At thirty-five and back on my own I knew better than to ask.

She stepped out of bed and reached for her clothes. Even standing still she looked like a dancer. She said, "I'll head for home, Reid."

"Sure." I bent and kissed her nose. I was fond of her, mysteries notwithstanding. She had helped me feel more like a person and less like a function, a computer print-out, ex-soldier, ex-detective on a city department, ex-husband, paid an impossibly small amount of money to keep law and order in Murphy's Harbour. The "Chief" was a joke. I was the entire force. Me, and Murphy, and Sam, my German shepherd.

4

I went downstairs and outside onto the cool predawn grass. Sam was on the prod, but he stopped very still as I spoke to him. "Okay, Sam, cool it. This is talking work, you can take it easy." He gave a low whine and fell flat, coiling down like an abandoned rope. I bumped the wire of the cage with the heel of my hand and went out to the car.

I passed what little there is to see in Murphy's Harbour on my way to the station. There's one main street with buildings onc side, water the other. The buildings include the rcal estate office and the beer store and the boardinghouses with their hand-lettered signs. There's a hardware and bait store and a grocery where they'll cook you a breakfast if you happen to be police chief. That's it. On the water side there's the Lakeshore tavern and the marina. Tonight the docks of the marina were crowded, about normal for mid-August.

The police office is a quarter mile out of town, on a swampy lot some councilor sold the township in the fifties. It's a concrete block building that looks too much like a bunker. There was a Mercedes out front with its headlights on. I drove up nose to nose, keeping my own lights on to check the occupants. Mr. Cottager and daughter. Him pale, her red-faced. He was a commuter and the family stayed here all summer.

He opened his door as I opened mine, and he cleared his throat as if it were all stuffed up with moncy. "Chief of Police?"

"Yeah."

"I hope this won't take long, it's late."

"I noticed." I walked by to the passenger side of the Mercedes. His daughter was sitting there, staring ahead like a hypnotized chicken. I broke the spell.

"Hi. I'm the police chief. I hear you did some lifooaving." Her father was fussing at my elbow. He was tense and it didn't take any working out. Young Sullivan, the fellow she'd pulled back into the boat, was the junior-grade stickman of the entire area. Papa wasn't happy that his daughter had been in that

5

boat, or worse, ashore on some island with Sullivan. He wanted this over, wiped off the record.

"Officer . . ." he said, and when I ignored him, "Chief . . ."

I said "yeah" again, starting to feel like Gary Cooper.

He did his throat-clearing bit again. "I can explain what happened."

"Great. You were in the boat as well?"

"Well no . . ."

I turned away. Murphy's Harbour is a tiny patch, but it's all mine and I don't have to put up with the kind of guys who run your life in a big department. I crouched a little and looked in at the kid who was watching us as if we were on television.

"Hi again. What's your name, please."

"Jane Bryant." There. She could talk as well as pull people into motorboats.

"Thank you, Jane. Can you tell me what happened?"

She looked past me quickly at her father, but his face was in shadow. She spoke up, nervously.

"We were in the boat, see."

Her father let up with the throat and started grinding his teeth. I felt for him. The kid was pretty and she must be smart. Maybe next year, when she was over sixteen, it wouldn't matter. Tonight it did.

She had to gather up her strength to talk over the tension he was generating. I turned to him and said, "You're making your daughter nervous, Mr. Bryant. Could you please stand back."

He backed off, as if he were pacing off the distance for a duel. The kid relaxed with every step he took. It didn't take police work to know that she and young Sullivan had been playing something a bit more strenuous than spin the bottle, and she figured her old man was going to lock up Sullivan for doing what comes naturally. I said, "The only thing I'm in-

6

terested in is what happened that made him fall out of the boat. Cool?"

It was. She took about a minute to give me what I wanted, the fact that they had run into something just east of Indian Island. Young Sullivan had been standing up on the seat of a little Fiberglas runabout his dumb father had laid on him for his sixteenth birthday. They ran into something at high speed and he flew over the top. The boat ran over him, but she managed to circle back and pick him up. There was a spatter of blood on her sleeve, an arc of spots that indicated he'd suffered arterial cuts. I was glad she had been there to help. Accidental death occurrences are a pain.

Her father had crept back while we talked, inching across the grass in front of the office like a turtle, until he was close enough to shut her up again. I told the girl, "Thanks, Jane. I'll just go take a look at what you hit." If I'd been young enough to want to prove something I'd have stepped back onto her father's toes and then apologized. Instead I said, "You've got a very brave daughter. She did a great job of lifesaving."

He cleared that throat of his again, and I could see his next move before he made it. He stuck his hand out in a handshake and awkwardly laid a bill in my hand. A sawbuck, I guessed. He was too full of his own importance to lay a twenty on me. I imagine he thought any policeman should be proud to frame a ten given him by J. Bryant, Esquire.

I didn't look at it, just reached out and stuffed it into his shirt pocket. "No need for that. This is my job."

He was alarmed. It was one thing to try and buy a copper, another to be held in contempt by one. "But this is just an acknowledgment that we appreciate your turning out late at night," he said.

"It comes with the uniform," I replied, and walked back to the cruiser.

I drove down to the main street, to the boathouse at the end

7

of the marina that held the police boat. We kept it locked to keep the vacationers from urinating in the gas tank or performing other antisocial acts that might prevent me from saving their necks when they fell out of their boats somewhere, as they did most weekends. I unlocked the door and climbed into the old eighteen-foot cedar strip. The boat was a joke, so far as patrolling went, but it was very forgiving; you could stand on the thwart to fish, or to pull in some gray-faced corpse as I had done once already this summer. The motor was a 20 Mercury, not big, but enough to purr the boat along at around fifteen miles an hour. It was a utility rig, and I was a utility police department, cheap enough that the taxpayers couldn't have gotten protection from the Ontario Provincial Police for the amount they paid me and Murphy.

The motor started with a smoky little burble. I pushed the choke home and backed out of the boathouse, into the midst of the weekenders' cruisers. Perhaps at high noon when the captains sat on their decks drinking gin and tonic with their lean, long-legged women, I might have envied them. But now, an hour before dawn, with the Big Dipper upside down in the sky and the bullfrogs twanging away along the shoreline, I was glad to be out and about. It was almost worth having quit the City Department.

I turned the boat up-channel, above the lock, and moved out at full power, fanning my flashlight over the water. If the girl was accurate in her placement of the thing they'd hit, it was a mile and a half away, drifting on a current that went nowhere at this time of year.

The beam of my light flattened itself over the bare brown rocks of the shoreline, where no cottages had sprouted. I settled back, figuring five minutes would see me on target. The wind of the boat's movement pierced my shirt and made me shudder. I was filled with a sudden sympathy for young Sullivan with his back and legs hanging in slices like bacon. I

8

didn't like the kid—he was too fast with his lip, too secure in daddy's money to take any notice of laws that weren't there to make life easy for him—but outboard cuts are ugly, spiral gashes all over the injured part. Then I grinned. If his back was cut, Fate might finally have gotten a piece of ass out of him for a change.

A mile upstream my light bounced back off something floating. It was a boat, as I'd thought. If it had stopped the Sullivan boat that quickly, it had to be big. And if he had gone over and then under his own boat, he had to have moved what he had hit. It was a fourteen-foot cedar strip, a workhorse fishing boat from one of the lodges or marinas along this stretch of the waterway.

I came alongside and grabbed the bowline, then cut my motor. I tied the bowline to my thwart and shone the light over the new boat. There were tackleboxes and two fishing rods in the bow. The rods were not set up. The boxes were closed. The side of the boat was sprung at the curve of the bow where something had hit it. There was no paint at the point of impact. That fit the facts. The Sullivan boat was Fiberglas.

I didn't stop to check anything more. It was getting chill with the predawn damp. I hitched the bowline of the boat around the handle of my motor and started up, taking care to keep the line clear of my propeller. Then I motored back toward the bright white light at the marina, my lodestar.

The world was quiet and I traveled in a tunnel of darkness, watching low to the water so I would not do the same as Sullivan had done. If he'd been sitting down, instead of standing there like a proud young rooster, he'd be in his own bed by now, and so would I. An old book title, *I Should Have Kissed Her More*, came to mind; if the little turd had been snuggling that girl he'd have been safe.

As I approached the dock I saw the man fishing. It looked

9

like a Picasso painting, a harlequin figure of blacks and whites made up of lighted portions of his body against the blackness of the shadows. I watched as the figure lifted a shaft of light and fanned it out gently toward mid-stream. I should have known Murphy would have come down to see what was happening. He would claim to be fishing, but you couldn't expect him to stay away from trouble. Not an old soldier like him.

As I came in, he set down the rod and moved out to dockside to meet me, moving slow and wonky on his metal leg. I cut the motor and tossed him my line. He pulled me in.

"Hi. Couldn't sleep, eh?"

Murphy spat into the water clear of the boat. "There's a goddamn pickerel out there, must be eight pounds. He feeds on the surface at night. I'm gonna get him."

"Sure," I said. I tied the stern line and got out of the boat. The second cedar strip bobbed up behind us, jackknifing gently as it hit.

Murphy reached down and grabbed it with his left hand, the one that's tied up into a knot from the same 88 shell that took his leg, on the Hitler Line in '44.

"Not too many cedar strips around anymore," he said.

"You know who owns it?"

He nodded. "Yeah."

I straightened up, shrugging my shoulders to try and get extra warmth from my thin shirt. "You gonna let me in on it?"

"Ross Winslow, from Ferry Beach Lodge."

I frowned. "It couldn't have floated into mid-channel from there. I wonder if somebody was out in it."

"What makes you think it was empty?"

I pointed at the fishing rods. "If a guy had gone fishing, the rods would have been set up. If he wasn't fishing, the rods wouldn't be in the boat."

Murphy did his old man thing with the dry throat. "Well, if

they were coming in from fishing, the rods would be down."

I shook my head. "There's no flashlight in the boat that I can see. They couldn't have taken down their rods in the dark."

We stood rolling these chunks of wisdom around in our heads like cannon balls. Then I yawned. "Well, the hell with it. I'm for bed. I'll check Winslow's place in the morning. See if any of his people were out late."

Murphy said, "Yeah, sure," and turned away.

I tied the Winslow boat and followed Murphy up the dock. "Come on, I'll drop you at the house."

He unsnapped his rod and folded it, then picked up his big old tackle box. "Thanks," he said bleakly. Both of us were tired.

I dropped him at the gate of his white-painted picture-book cottage with the honest-to-God roses around the door. Their scent was as heavy as sadness on the air. He said nothing, just nodded a thank you as I started back to my house. The bed was still fragrant from Linda's perfume, which was lighter and sweeter than those sad purple roses of Murphy's.

2

Murphy rang me at seven. I was already awake, looking at the reflection of the sunlight on the walls of my room. It's not much of a room—the wallpaper was put up when Queen Victoria had her picture on the money and there are cracks in the ceiling—but the light patterns made me feel happy. Until Murphy called.

"I phoned Winslow and there's no answer."

I rolled my legs off the edge of the bed and stretched my back. "Listen, he's a big boy. He's also the randiest bachelor in the goddamn township. Dollars to doughnuts he's in the sack with one of his guests."

Murphy doesn't panic easily. But you can't shake his opinions either.

"I've known Ross ever since he joined my platoon as a reinforcement in Italy during the war. He's at work around the place by seven, gets up at six, no matter where he's been the night before."

I frowned into the phone. It wasn't usual for Murph to sound this upset. The only time I'd ever seen him lose his cool was when we pulled in the child that had drowned while the parents were drinking in their room. Other than that he would have made a good policeman. He wasn't, because of his injuries, but he ran the office and carried out more police work than most city coppers, so I usually went with his hunches.

"Listen. I'll grab some breakfast and head over there to chase him up. Okay?"

"Okay," he said grudgingly, and hung up.

I slipped on an old pair of swim trunks and went downstairs. Sam was lying at the door of his pen. As always, he'd been ready five minutes before I showed.

I let him out and rolled him over to pat his stomach. He's a big black and tan German shepherd, a show dog with brains. He's half my police strength and all the family I've got, so we get on well.

I let him run for a minute or two, then I went down to the dock. He trotted after me. I gave a short whistle and he sat.

I dived in. The water was cold and I squeezed tighter into my skin as I dived, hoarding my warmth while the light grew gray and dim. When I came to the end of my breath I surfaced. Sam was still sitting, like a statue. I gave another whistle, of a different length this time. Instantly he bounded in after me and paddled out. I dived under him and came up on the far side. He turned in the water and followed. I dived again.

When our game tired me out I swam to the shore and walked out. Sam came charging out after me, barreling up the beach and shaking himself with delight. I patted him again and went and took his dish from the dog run. He tailed me as I padded into the kitchen and mixed his breakfast, dog meal and an egg and some oil. He sat when I put the dish down and waited until I gave him the okay.

I dressed in uniform pants and a clean shirt, ate my own

13

breakfast, then fastened my gun belt and went out toward the car. Sam followed. I opened the rear door for him and he leaped inside, then coiled down on the seat.

When we parked outside the station I indicated to Sam with a flick of my head that he should follow. He came over the front seat like smoke and waited beside me as I shut the door. Murphy was already in the office, at his desk with its tall stool that was made specially to keep his bad leg straight. He frowned at me over the report he was typing as we entered. I looked around at my empire. It's small. Aside from the type-writer that Murphy was clip-clopping at with his good hand, there are a couple of desks and file cabinets, a teletype machine, and a gun rack with a Winchester pump and a Remington .308 rifle chained into it. The front of the office has a counter at belly height. At the back of the room is another door that leads out to our cells, two of them, and the corridor where we make out the arrest reports when I bring someone in, which is rarely.

Murphy nodded, not speaking.

"Did you phone your old buddy again?" I asked him.

He nodded again.

"Listen, don't talk my ear off, eh. I'll take his boat back and ask him what happened, all right?"

"Yeah. Makes sense," he said. He had hardly looked up from his report and I knew it wasn't that important, nothing in Murphy's Harbour was that important. Except perhaps a missing friend who had been against the Hitler Line with you when you were both young and whole and full of courage.

I went over to the teletype. It's tied into the Ontario Provincial Police circuit. We get anything the OPP broadcasts province-wide. Aside from that we wait for phone calls for anything special such as a wide load coming down our section of the Trans-Canada. "Anything new?"

"Not on that." Murphy sniffed. "Could be trouble, though.

14

I was listening to the weather on the radio. They said it's a good weekend. Everyone's heading north."

"Standard for August."

"Yeah, but they reported from their chopper that the Devil's Disciples are coming up, a big knot of the hairy bastards on their motorbikes."

"They probably won't stop here," I said.

"Not with you around they won't." His envy was in his voice. He didn't condemn me. He understood about bullies. He understood about killing as well, killing that happens reflexively when a man has been trained to do it instinctively if presented with the proper stimuli.

"They don't know I'm working here," I said.

"What if they do, and they pull in here when you're out?" He was serious about it. He looked at me straight now, out of deep blue Irish eyes, only they seldom smiled.

"You use the necessary amount of force to stop them wrecking the place," I said, taking out my key ring and unlocking the chain on the guns. I took down the pump and worked the action. A fat brass-butted shell presented itself. Now I had to unload it to prevent a shell from being in the chamber. I pumped it five times, catching the heavy shells as they flew.

"There. Five shots of SSG makes you the equal of a whole herd of rounders."

I started stuffing the purple shells back into the magazine. Each one held eight lead balls capable of bringing down a deer, or a man. Murphy was safe. And so was Murphy's Harbour.

"Relax. If they stake out the OK Corral, call me." I winked at him. He didn't return it, and I walked out with Sam a tight six inches from my left heel.

It was busy at the marina. George Horn, the Indian kid who works the pumps, was filling two cruisers simultaneously and carrying on a conversation with a third guy who was waiting with an empty outboard motor tank.

He saw me and waved, then loped down the dock to meet me. "Hey, Reid, you bring in Winslow's boat last night?"

I guess I ought to be fussy about being called chief, but a copper never has many friends and George was useful.

"You know it's Winslow's boat?"

He nodded, slim and young and right. "No doubt about it. That's his Evinrude."

"That's what Murph says. I found it in mid-channel up by Indian Island, after young Sullivan creamed it."

George grinned. "Yeah, I heard. He was laying that Bryant girl."

I was glad I hadn't accepted daddy's sawbuck.

"Not right then he wasn't. He hit the boat and flew out." George paused to work out the sexual possibilities of falling out of the boat while otherwise occupied than in watching where you were going. He frowned.

I started my interrogation. "So how come you know his motor?" George held up one finger then darted off and took money from his customers. I waited, looking at the boat. What I saw made me whistle with surprise. Sam sat up straight, puzzled. I told him "Easy!" and waited for George to come back. He was talking as he ran.

"He was here last night when I closed down. Working on the motor. Said the plug was fouled."

"Was it running bad when he got here?"

George shook his head. "No. Running good. I wondered why he was fooling with it."

"Anybody with him? A broad maybe?"

He grinned again with the confidence of a boy whose whole life revolves around his sexuality. "Hell, Reid, it wouldn't have been his plug he was taking out, would it?"

"Kids. No respect for their elders." I let him have his smile,

16

then dropped the bomb on him. "Did anybody cut the lines to the motor since this morning?"

He glanced at me, then into the boat, his chin dropping in surprise. "Hey no. I never seen that happen."

I got down into the boat and checked it thoroughly, as I should have done the night before. The feed line from the tank to the motor had been slashed. There was no trace of the spilled gasoline that must have been in the rubber bulb when it was cut. It had happened hours ago, perhaps back before the boat drifted out and got in Sullivan's way. There were three life jackets tucked under the bow in case the boat was stopped by a law officer, namely me. Two fishing rods, not set up. A big tackle box and a box of worms. They had been there long enough to go dry. They stank. I tipped them over the side and a flutter of little sunfish rose and dimpled the water as they caught the free feed. I was more puzzled now. The boat could never have been driven without the line to the motor. And people did not leave their tackle boxes in their boats. Tackle vanished, even in a law-abiding place like Murphy's Harbour.

George was watching me, waiting for me to come up with an answer like the high priced executive I was supposed to be.

I said, "I guess I'll go see if he's at home."

He looked disappointed. Like maybe he had expected me to come on like Sherlock Holmes. I don't do much of that. No policeman does. Certainly not many small-town coppers with nobody to back their hunches.

I gathered the bow line of the Winslow boat and got into the police boat. Sam came behind me and lay down on the floorboards, out of the way. That dog was so well trained he even knew how far forward to sit.

The motor started at once. George cast me off and waved. I waved back, once, and set off across the bay toward the abandoned ferry boat that gave Winslow's place its name. There

17

were children swimming off the dock beside the boat. As I came in they jumped off and swam out to the raft that Winslow had moored for them. I cut the motor and slid in, Winslow's boat coming up fast to bump me as I stopped. The kids watched, brown and silent.

I tied up both boats and walked down the dock toward the lodge building. It was a single-story building with a kitchen, a small cafe area, and a rec room. At one end was Winslow's private quarters. Around it, in a semicircle, up on the rocks, were the cottages he rented for a living, a thin living.

There were a couple of families out on the wiry grass in front of their cottages. And drawn up on the sand in front of the cafe were two elderly sedans with the kind of paintwork that shouts "a teenager owns me."

As I came up to the coffee shop the door burst open and four youths came out, fast enough that they didn't want to meet me, slow enough that I had no real reason to stop their going. I watched them climb into the sedans and spurt back over the sand, off up the road that led to the highway. I made a mental note of their numbers. I'd only been in this job for three months, but there was something a little alien about the way those kids had left. When I knew the area better, I'd maybe know what they were doing here. I filed their presence in my head beside the numbers and the fact that Winslow probably didn't get very fat running this place.

As I was about to go into the coffee shop, a girl came running down from the rocks. She was dressed in city clothes, a tan skirt with a slit in it, and a blouse that was too floppy to go well with suntan lotion. And she was running hard, not doing the elbows-and-knees-out swing that most women use when they want you to see how they run. I waited and she panted up to me. She was blond, maybe thirty, one twenty, something of a looker if you like them tall and slender.

She said, "I was just going to call you."

"Something the matter?"

She began to speak, then drew a great gulp of air to steady herself. "I don't know," she said. I must have looked skeptical because she reached out impulsively and covered my hand with both of hers. "I don't know for sure, officer. But I'm worried."

Behind her the families at the cottages had gathered in a single circle, like Indians in a B movie.

"Is someone missing?"

She nodded, tight mouthed, not speaking. I took pity on her, with the gallery staring into her soul, and led her out on the dock where it was quieter. I indicated the bow of the police boat. "Sit down and tell me what's on your mind." She turned and sat, the boat dipping discreetly under her. Sam looked at her curiously. I nodded to him and he came out of the boat. She looked at Sam, then at me. Her face was pale. If she was on vacation, this was her first day. And there were dark circles under her eyes.

"I'm not sure if they are missing," she said awkwardly.

"Who are *they*?" Police questions always sound dumb to the person who's answering them, but you have to remember that we don't have anything until we've asked a few obvious things.

She thought about her answer for so long that I began to think she hadn't been listening. As I was about to try again she said, "Two people. Derek Pardoe and Mr. Murray."

"What makes you think they're missing?" This was going to be a Dick and Jane investigation, I could tell. See Dick, see Jane. Does Jane know where Dick has gone?

"They've been gone all night."

"So when did you see them last?"

"Around ten, maybe a little earlier, it was just dark." Her voice was starting to choke and it looked as if I'd be handing her the Kleenex before we were much further along.

"Where was that, here?"

She shook her head, almost angrily, whipping her hair like tiny gold lashes. "No, in the little town, across the way there." She waved at Murphy's Harbour, struggling to be seen, three-quarters of a mile away over the channel. My hair started to tingle. I felt the beginning of a case. It was good, like that first jolt that lets you know a pickerel has grabbed your jig and is mouthing it for a moment to see if he wants to end up over your mantelpiece.

"And they took off in a boat."

She frowned at me. "How did you know that?"

"People take boats a lot from the marina."

"I didn't say it was at the marina." She seemed wary.

I stood up straight and did my yokel number, humble but sincere. "We aren't going to find out anything if you don't give me the facts now, are we?"

She thought about that and said, "I see" in a grudging tone that could have meant anything.

"Now. Were they alone?"

"No. The boat man was with them."

"Was it Mr. Winslow?" A newcomer like her wouldn't know his first name.

"That's right."

"And they were heading over here?"

She shook her head again, just as violently, then stopped suddenly as if she was giving too much away. "I don't know where they were going."

"Then why are you here?"

She pursed her mouth and looked down at her fingers. "I knew his name so I found out where he lived and came over this morning."

"And did you come to Murphy's Harbour to meet Mr. Winslow?"

"No." The shake again. She must be as rigid as hell, prob-

20

ably some kind of cashier or teller, I thought, someone who dealt with certainties all the time.

She became aware of her attitude and toned it down. "No, we just met up with him at the marina and he offered to take Derek and Mr. Murray where they had to go."

"After dark, leaving you on the dock? That's kind of late to go calling, isn't it?"

She fenced, giving me a half answer. "I could have gone with them but I was tired from the drive, and Derck wanted me to go to the motel at the highway. . . ." She waved back vaguely over her shoulder.

"How far had you driven?"

"From New York."

The way she clipped it I knew she meant Manhattan, but I stayed in character. "The city or the state?"

"The city."

"Okay. Now who had you driven all the way from New York to visit?"

She stood up, leaving the boat curtseying idly. "I don't have to tell you that. I want you to report that Mr. Pardoe is missing."

A lot of things were coming together. Pardoe was her lover. She wouldn't have switched from familiar to formal and back that way if he wasn't. And she was infinitely more concerned about him than she was about the other guy, Murray.

I kept right on being reasonable. "If you tell me where they might have gone, I'll have a place to start looking for them, right?"

She shook her head, slowly this time, fighting with herself about what she was to do. "No," she said at last. "Derek told me not to tell anyone."

I didn't say anything. It was a waste of time pushing her at this stage. It might be unnecessary anyway. If they'd fallen out of the boat when Sullivan clipped it, they were going to wash down to the lock later on this weekend. The lockkeeper would drag them out and call me. I said, "Okay, then, let's start with the unclassified stuff. Like what your name is."

"Angela Masters."

I took out my notebook and wrote it down. "All right, Miss Masters, what are the full names of the other people?"

She said, "Derek Pardoe."

"How old?"

She had no hesitation. "Thirty-two."

"How big a man is he?"

She shrugged, an upturn of her shoulders and hands that looked studied, but wasn't. I added the fact to the file I was building on her. Probably European stock, despite the Brit-sounding name. Limeys don't turn their shoulders inside out.

"Is he your size, my size, what?"

For a moment she forgot herself, became a measuring tape, standing tall, jutting her breasts as she measured herself against me. "I'd say he was right in between." I'm six one, she was six inches shorter. I wrote "five ten."

"How about build?"

We got through it all eventually. I got a picture of a slim, pale guy of medium height, wearing a tan business suit with a striped shirt and red spotted tie. All it told me was that he must have stood out like a banner in church among the blue jeans and the open-necked shirts of Murphy's Harbour. She hadn't told me what his job was. And she didn't.

Murray was easier. I got the kind of description you pick up after a robbery. He was heavy-set, red-faced, forty to forty-five. Check suit, green shirt, green tie. But she had to work to get any of the facts out of her memory. She wasn't interested, that much was obvious. Pardoe was her man.

I closed the book and pointed to Winslow's boat. "Does that look like the boat they got into?" She went up and stared into it as if it were a book of mug shots. She was in profile and I had to admit she was a looker. She had the tip-tilted nose of Eastern Europe, good forehead, firm breasts. Pardoe was a lucky man. Or had been, twenty-four hours ago.

She turned back to me, shaking her head in concern. "I don't know. I don't know anything about boats. It could have been."

I changed the tack. "Had they been drinking?"

She looked shocked. "No, of course not."

"It's not a frivolous question. This is vacation country, people drink."

"Not Derek." She shook her head again. "He was here on serious business."

I said, "Oh?"

She looked at me quickly, then looked away, angry with herself. "I already told you, he was here to see someone."

"Yes, you did," I agreed. "But you didn't say who, or why."

She gave a little gasping sob and then checked herself. "I can't. I promised I wouldn't. He told me people would ask."

"Is he in some kind of trouble?"

"Trouble?" She almost laughed. "Derek never did anything wrong in his whole life."

Great, I thought, just what we need. A missing saint. I said, "Listen, this is unpleasant for you, what say we go in and get a cup of coffee." She sniffed a couple of times and dashed her cuff across her eyes. Then she blinked and nodded.

I led her back, past the silent group of watchers. Perhaps they were waiting for me to put the handcuffs on her, something, anything to avoid the boredom of another sunny day of kids and swimming and drinks with the people next door. Even on holiday, people don't relax that much.

We reached the wooden screen door and I yanked on it, lifting the ancient flatiron that hung on a cord over the jamb, automatic door closer, early Ontario style. Inside was the standard greasy-spoon lodge kitchen. The Ministry of Tourism at Queen's Park in Ontario would like it if every resort had haute cuisine. Most of them are like this, plastic-topped counter with chrome stools and plastic seats, leaking wood wool. Two tables that needed wiping and kitchen chairs that looked as if too many kids had leaned back on them too many times. On the walls were pictures of fish taken years ago in this reach of the water. And on the wall behind the counter, where the coffee machine and the four-slot toaster were drawing flies, there were pictures of the native dishes: blueberry pie with ice cream, Coca-Cola, hamburgers with the works. Sissie Lowrie was standing behind the counter, cigarette dangling from the corner of her mouth. She managed to make a clean white apron look slovenly. I said, "Hi, Sis, got a couple of coffees?"

She sniffed and picked up the institution-style mugs from behind the counter. "Sure do, Reid. You lookin' for Ross the boss?"

I walked through the little lift-up flap at the end of the counter, motioning the girl to follow. "In a manner of speaking. Mind if we sit out back?"

"Help yourself." She jerked her head backward toward the doorway of the kitchen and drew a couple of coffees, slopping some in both saucers.

I led the way out back. It was warm, an unhealthy indoor warmth filled with steamy chili smells and the hot metallic aroma of the big wood stove they had never replaced.

Sissie brought the coffee, carefully not getting any ash in it. I took them both, handing one to the girl, who took it as if she was expecting me to hand her a prize for good behavior. "Seen Ross today?" I asked Sissie.

She crossed her arms and gave her brassiere a quick boost before blowing the ash off her cigarette and answering. "Nary a sign of the old bastard."

"When'd you start?"

"Eight o'clock, on the nail." There was a touch of pride in the way she said it. I guessed that she and her husband had gone their usual bout with John Barleycorn the night before, but it hadn't, by God, stopped her from climbing out of bed and making it to her job on time.

"Is he generally in when you get here?"

She nodded. "Never known him missing. Not in fourteen years." She laid the number on our heads like a prayer.

I sipped my coffee and set it down. Angela Masters was still holding hers as if waiting for one of us to explain how to use it. "He was seen last night at the marina, around ten, with a couple of other fellers."

She shook her head, disbelieving. "Don't sound like Ross. That ain't where he spends his Fridays."

"This lady saw him there," I said.

She shook her head again, dislodging more flakes of gray tobacco ash from her butt. "Must've been somebody else. Ten o'clock, Ross is in the beverage room. And you wouldn't see him with two other guys unless his girl had a couple o' sisters."

The girl set down her coffee and crossed her hands in front of her, the way a man does when he's been punched in the gut. "Are you telling me that this Mr. Winslow is a womanizer?" she asked icily.

I said nothing. Sissie did it for me. She dropped her butt on the floor and tramped it with a size nine. "He don't give me no trouble," she said. Nor would he unless she lost sixty pounds and got herself a full set of teeth, I thought. To the girl I said, "Ross is kind of a local character. That's what makes it odd that he'd be at the marina on a Friday night. It makes the whole thing unusual."

She was angry. Her voice was low but there were white pinch marks on either side of her nose. She looked through me for close to a minute and when I didn't drop my eyes said, "You know more about this than you're saying, don't you?"

25

"Not a lot," I said honestly. "I have a boat, could have belonged to Ross Winslow. Two kids found it floating, abandoned, last night. Now you say two other people are missing. I wonder what's happening."

She stood up from her wooden chair, trembling with anger. "You mean that boat was found last night and you're just now getting around to investigating it?" She paced up and down, a few strides each way like a sentry, banging her fists against her sides. I thought that she must have seen a lot of plays in her time. I waited for the next line. It was predictable. "What's your number? I'm going to report you to your superiors."

Sissie laughed. "Save your breath, kid. Reid here's the whole damn department, him 'n that dog of his."

The girl did not back off. She hissed at me with rage. "Well, why aren't you doing something constructive, instead of sitting here drinking coffee?"

I sipped and said, "Sometimes the best way to save time is to use a little. Like now, I know there were three men in the boat, not just one. It isn't likely they all three fell overboard. So it seems to me that they're up at the place this Mr. Pardoe came here to visit. Right this minute they're probably finishing the bacon and eggs, laughing and scratching and thinking of heading back home."

She said nothing. She was smart enough to know I was right, on the facts she had given me. She wanted more from me, but was not going to pay for it with more information. I prodded anyway.

"So why don't you tell me who they were calling on. Then I'll go on up there and we'll sort this thing out." She shook her head. I watched her do it, then set down my coffee cup. "Thanks for the java, Sis. I'm heading back to the office. If anybody comes in with some news about Ross, give me a call."

This shook the girl. She grabbed my arm. Suddenly I wasn't a bum. I was wearing a white hat and I had a splendid white

26

charger under me. I was going to save her. "Don't go back to your office," she begged. Her irises were the color of bottle glass and her perfume was fresh and sweet. "Please, if you know this area, come and look for them, in the boat. They must be stranded somewhere."

I didn't answer at once. I wanted her to give me a hint, but I didn't want her along with me. Not if I was liable to be pulling in a puffy gray corpse with water running out of the nose and mouth.

Sissie Lowrie came in on my side. "I don't think you should go," she said with sudden maternal softness. "It'll be . . . it'll be cold in that boat."

"Cold?" the girl almost shrieked. "Cold? Today?"

"Just tell me where they were going?" I asked.

She hesitated, forcing herself to stop and consider. For a moment the penny in her mind was teetering on its rim. Then it clanged down. "I can't do that," she said, but without real firmness. I could see Sissie Lowrie's interest growing. This was the most exciting thing that had happened to her since her husband's gas station caught fire in 1946. She was opening her mouth to speak and at the same moment the phone rang, the sound seeming almost to fall out of her mouth.

She turned away and picked up the phone. "Ferry Beach," her voice yodeled upward. She was almost a teenager again in her involvement. She turned and looked at me, her eyes widening. "Yes, he's here . . ." She handed me the phone like a bowling trophy. "Murphy, for you."

I took it. "Yeah, Murph."

"I'm at the lock house. A body just washed down. Jack Collins called me. We just pulled it out."

"Is it Ross?" I knew it wasn't. He would have named Ross. It had to be one of this young woman's two men. I could feel the pulse jumping in my throat. Good-bye parking tickets. I had myself a piece of honest-to-god police work.

Murphy's voice was surprisingly eager. He was as mystified

27

as me. "No. This guy's a stranger. Big, heavy-set, around forty-five, I'd say, black hair. I get the feeling he could've been a drinker."

"That sounds like a man called Charles Murray. There's a woman here says he and Ross and a man called Pardoe went off in Ross's boat last night, around ten."

Murphy cleared his throat, like a log being dragged over gravel. "Tell me, did she say what line of work this Murray was in?" He was angling, I could feel it.

"No. Why?"

The same growl again, then he said, "Well, the reason I'm asking is he's carrying a .38 Smith and Wesson."

3

Word had gotten around.

By the time I made it back to town with Angela Masters in her Volvo, there must have been fifty people around the front of McKenney's funeral parlor. None of them was grieving. Grooving would be closer to their state of mind. Most of them had cans of pop they'd bought down at Ellicott's store, and a couple had radios, tuned to different rock stations. There was a whole lot of laughing and shoving going on. One or two of the girls put on a serious face for my sake, but it wasn't real. Nothing livens up a long hot day like the death of a stranger. I guessed one of them must have been at the lock when the body came bumping down. One scream had gathered all the idlers for half a mile each way.

Maybe once I would have tried to shoo them all off, all the gum-snapping crowd of them. But it was a waste of time. And in a minor way, I felt for them. After you've seen enough guys left where they dropped, just the dog tags picked up by their buddies, you stop worrying about death. It is an unpleasant fact of life and it sure as hell makes a break in the routine.

I pulled into the driveway alongside the funeral parlor, the girl got out, and I opened the rear door and gave Sam the nod. He followed us in through the wide door they use for shipping out the coffins, into the back part of the building where Mc-Kenney does his dreary, necessary business.

I told the girl to sit down and went on through the double doors into McKenney's preparation room. Murphy was there, towering over McKenney, a little pink and white guy in a black suit. He has gray hair and a suitably sorrowful expression that keeps his mouth closed over the worst set of false teeth I've ever seen. When I came in he parted his Chiclets in a grin.

"Hello, Chief," he whispered. "Did you bring someone to identify the deceased?"

"Yeah. Let her sit outside a minute, Jack, while I talk to Murph."

"Whatever you say," he cooed.

Murphy was looking down at the body. He turned and said, "He looks drowned, Reid, but he took one goddawful crack on the head. Come 'n' see."

I checked the gray face. Down the left temple the skin was split, pulled back obscenely, revealing colorless flesh underneath, water bleached like fish meat.

"Did the doctor see him?"

Murphy nodded. "Just for a couple of minutes. He was heading out for a delivery. He said it took priority over this."

"I guess so." I pointed to the gash. "Did he have anything to say about that?"

"Figures it could have been caused by banging the head against the thwart of the boat when it was hit. He's not sure if it killed him right off or if he drowned. Said he'll do an autopsy later if you want him to."

I sniffed. "Sure looks drowned, doesn't he?"

McKenney chimed in softly. "A few hours in the water will do that, Chief."

I guess I could like him better if he was less sneaky about his trade. I said nothing, just rolled the flap of the coat back on the left side to reveal the leather holster and the pistol. "Did you search him?" I asked.

"I figured that was your job," Murphy said, a touch of bitterness in his voice. The chief before me had been older than Murphy and had left most of the dirty work to him. I'd made it clear I wanted things done my way.

"Thanks. Let's see if he's got any reason for carrying that thing."

I lifted the body slightly, enough to reach the hip pocket. It was tight to him; the body had swollen and the suit seemed to have shrunk. He had a billfold in there. It was wet and repellant. I inched it out with my fingertips, flipped it open, and saw it contained a big brass badge, an ornate shield design. The words "Bonded Security Service Operator 376" were picked out in chrome. The badge looked like it came in a box of Crackerjack, but it was probably from a real security firm. Some of those companies are chintzy beyond belief.

I opened the compartments in the wallet and found a hundred and fifty-six dollars in U.S. bills. "Fifteen consecutive tens," I said aloud. "Looks as if he drew a yard and a half of expense money for this trip."

"He's left it a bit late to spend any of it." Murphy barked out a quick laugh.

I smiled politely and went on searching. There was a driver's license made out in the name of Charles Murray, with an address in New York City.

"He must have come here on business," Murphy said, as if apologizing for losing his head and laughing earlier.

The holster had bothered me so I checked it again. The snap was made of heavy leather with a big clip that was stiff and difficult to open; I tried it a couple of times.

"Was the snap open like this when you found him?"

"Yeah. Doesn't look like it came undone by accident. It takes a good pull to open it," Murphy said. He was standing with his bad hand pressed under his other armpit, the way he always did when he was thinking hard.

I figured he was coming to the same conclusion I'd already reached. This man had been going for his gun when whoever it was clobbered him in the temple. I locked eyes with him and frowned slightly. This was not information for McKenney to play with.

McKenney wasn't paying attention, not that you could notice. He had tiptoed to the door and peeked out at the Masters girl. Now he came back, his thin little lips parted over those incredible teeth. "Do you think we should do the identification?"

I nodded. "Sure. Get a sheet to throw over this guy and we'll wheel him out there for her to see."

"You mean you won't bring her in here?" He was upset. This was his studio. His works of art originated here.

"She may not be part werewolf," I told him. "Places like this give a lot of people the creeps. Let's do it in the hallway." He gave a tiny pout and took the rail at the end of the slab to wheel it through the doorway like a grocery cart full of provisions.

"Throw a sheet over him, eh?" I repeated.

He bridled at this. "It'll get wet."

"And it'll dry." I told him, "I don't want this woman spooked—she's the only one who knows what the hell is going on." We went out: McKenney with the trolley, then Murphy, good hand holding his good leg like a man going up a steep hill; then me. The girl stared at us as if we were the school tough guys coming to pull her hair.

I squatted down to her eye level. "Miss Masters, I'm certain this is Mr. Murray, not your friend Mr. Pardoe. But if it's neither one of them, we can save a lot of upset at somebody's

house tonight if you'll please identify the man on the trolley."
She looked at me, her eyes widening in a way that would have
been sexy, provocative, in any other setting. Her mouth was
tightly shut. "So I'm going to pull the sheet back and ask you
'Is this the man you knew as Mr. Murray?' If it is, you just nod
your head."

She gave me a tiny nod and I straightened up and took her
elbow. She rose with me and stared down at the sheet. I could
see McKenney looking her up and down. Whether he was
leching or just sizing her up for one of his empty boxes, his
heart was in it, I could tell.

I took the corner of the sheet and pulled it down from the
face. I had already turned the head so she saw the unbroken
temple. "Is this the man you knew as Charles Murray?"

She nodded. "That's Mr. Murray," she said resolutely. I
flipped the sheet back over the dead gray face and took her
more firmly by the elbow. "Thank you, Miss Masters. Now
I'm going to take you back to your motel, where you can rest
up."

"Thank you," she said in a diminishing voice.

"There are a few more things I have to do first," I told her.
"If you'd be kind enough to wait here. Mr. McKenney will get
you a glass of water if you'd like one." I wanted him out of the
way while I talked to Murph. You might as well take an ad
in the local paper as try to carry out a private investigation in
a small town. Gossip is the currency, and as far as I could tell
McKenney was a regular customer for it.

He trotted off obediently for water and I took Murphy back
inside, wheeling the corpse with me. "Couple more things,
Murph. Who found him?"

"Jack Collins at the lock. He would've come over here but
somebody has to stay on duty."

"Okay, I'll stop by later and get a statement. Also, the doctor; when's he coming back?"

"Around three." Murphy was tightening up on me. The mystery of Ross Winslow took priority over this body.

McKenney came back, clearing his throat discreetly, a little birdy kind of noise. "What about the deceased, Reid? What do I do about him?"

"Nothing yet. Don't do anything rash like burying him; the next of kin may have other plans."

McKenney humphed, a civil servant's sound of displeasure. I said to Murph, "First thing, call his head office and give them the glad tidings. Second, search him thoroughly. See what all he's carrying and find out why he's carrying it."

"I brought some property envelopes from the station," Murphy said. He was rolling a cigarette as we talked, moving like a Hollywood cowboy, doing it all with his one good hand. When he finished and stuck the ragged smoke between his lips I struck a match for him. He inhaled greedily, sucking down the smoke in a great puff that burned up a quarter inch of his cigarette. "Thanks," he said shortly.

"Try and find out what he was doing up here. It could be he was just playing cowboys and Indians with that goddamn gun."

"Doubt it," Murphy said, closing one eye to avoid the drift of his smoke. "If it's their gun I'll bet he had to check it when he was off duty."

"You do in the police department," I said automatically. Murphy and McKenney both looked at me, wondering if I was going to open up about the bikies, but I changed the subject. "I think we ought to contact the scuba club. If he was in the boat when the Sullivan kid hit it, there's a chance we can expect two more bodies to wash down."

"I already phoned them," Murphy said carefully.

I reached out and bumped him on the shoulder, the way I might have patted Sam. "Hang loose, Murph; Ross Winslow is alive and well somewhere."

34

"Maybe," he said.

I ignored McKenney, handing Murphy the only crumb of hope I had. "I didn't tell you, did I? The Winslow boat had been put out of action. The fuel lines were cut. I figure it must have been drifting before Sullivan's kid hit it."

Murphy took his cigarette out of his mouth and looked at the end as if the answer might be written there. "What in hell is going on?" he asked at last, not looking up.

I felt sorry for him. He'd had thirty years of pain and limitation as a result of the war and now the only guy who understood him or remembered the action was missing, maybe drowned. His thin old shoulders were rounded with the weight of it. "I'm going to take this woman back to her place, then go upstream and see if I can find out where Ross has gone. I'll check some cottages. Some of the people who fish up further might have seen him, or this guy Pardoe." He didn't answer and I asked him, "You going to be okay, with the search and the phone calls?"

He dropped his cigarette end and put his good foot on it. McKenney gave a little hiss of disgust at this abuse of his tiles. "I'll be fine, as long as nothing else comes up," Murphy said.

"Like what?"

"Well, there's that gang of bikies, they could pull in any time for a reunion with you."

"They won't," I told him, but he only looked at me out of narrow blue eyes.

"I couldn't handle them without help," he admitted.

"So okay. I'll leave Sam with you. He could take on the entire gang on his own."

Now he relaxed, his face falling into the creases of an old grin. "I b'lieve I'd rather have him than a company of infantry."

"Done." I stooped and patted Sam, looking into his eyes. "Good dog. Stay with Murph!"

I straightened up and Murphy said, "Come, Sam." Sam trotted to him and he said, "Good boy, sit." Sam sat, ignoring me.

I went out, past the girl sitting there, dry eyed, holding her glass of water. "Come on, Miss Masters," I said. "I'll take you back to your motel."

The crowd was still waiting outside, and they had gotten louder. I figured somebody had made a trip to the liquor store for a couple of mickies of rye. I walked up and took the radio out of the hand of a kid who was dancing to it, a big corn-fed boy with a summer tan and too much softness around the face and shoulders. I pressed the off switch.

"That's better," I said cheerfully. "There's nothing to see here. Please get on about your business. It's too nice a day to hang around funeral parlors." The kid started to bluster, but I looked through his eyes, into the back of his skull, and smiled.

He'd heard about my battles. They all had. He dropped his eyes and turned away. "Okay, killer," he said over his shoulder.

I said nothing. I stood there, airing my smile until they all went away, still in a group, down toward the dock of the marina. They would soon disperse. It was hot and the water was more inviting than the dusty main street where nothing was happening anymore.

I got into the car. The girl was sitting in the passenger side with all the windows up. It was hot and there was a faint aroma of her perfume and unemptied ashtrays. I wound down my window and asked her, "Where to?"

"The Canadiana, up on the highway."

I knew the place. It specialized in the hot pillow trade, except in midsummer when genuine moms and pops kept the rooms full. "It ain't fancy, but it's home," I said. She began to laugh. It started out as a little squeak of amusement but it turned into giggles and then into sobbing. I looked sideways at her. Her shoulders were heaving and I knew she needed more help than I could give her with chitchat. I drove off, past the gang of kids who had just left the funeral parlor. One or two of the bolder ones called things out at us. "Way to go, killer" was the one that stood out. I noticed the kid who said it and scored him in my mind for the next time he wanted to park illegally. It was hard enough to live down what I'd done, even without the wisecracks.

When I reached the police office, I stopped the car. "Wait here," I told her. She took no notice. Her head was bowed, blond hair spilling into her lap as her shoulders shook. I let myself into the office and unlocked the evidence cupboard. I was back outside in thirty seconds, holding a bottle of scotch in the brown paper bag the Ontario Liquor Commission uses for gift wrapping.

I drove away from the office fast, doing it on purpose to jolt her physically out of her misery. It worked. She began the organic business of survival, looking up first, then grabbing hold of the dash with one hand as I pulled the car around the bends of our side road.

She still hadn't spoken when we pulled up to the tacky sign of the Canadiana, but I knew she was at least capable of it. I wheeled in front of the office and slowed. "Which unit?"

"Four," she said nervously. She was back in control of herself. I thought my job might almost be easy.

I pulled up in front of unit four. It was a prefab cabin, looking more like a B-movie set than a piece of real accommodation. "We're home," I said, and she got out of the car without a word. I picked up the brown paper bag and followed, hoping that Mike Higgins, who ran the place, was out back somewhere. Policemen don't customarily take good looking blondes to motels at high noon, not holding bottles they don't, not in a small town.

I stood in the doorway and checked the interior. There was nothing to help me. One double bed, rumpled. Lime-green nylon nightgown. Two suitcases. One pale blue, open. One tan, closed. His and hers. Only he hadn't been here last night.

The girl watched me as if I were a magician at her birthday party.

"Sit down," I suggested. And when she was slow to move, "Please." She sat. I went into the bathroom, collected two thick old tumblers, and slipped the scotch out of the bag. It was an expensive brand, the bottle almost full. I'd caught the driver before he'd even finished his seduction.

She looked up at me when I reentered the bedroom, her eyes narrowing a little. I wondered if she thought I was bush enough to make a pass at her. I poured a stiff one and closed the bottle. "Drink it," I said.

"Like that?" There was a world of experience in her voice. A lot of men had poured her a lot of drinks, I figured.

"Want some water with it?"

"Please." She was almost back to normal, still in shock enough to take the drink, but not so fragile as she had been.

I brought water in the other glass and mixed her drink until she nodded, as mindlessly as if we were children playing dolly's tea parties. I handed it to her and she did a little automatic smile, the kind that women give when they sit down sideways on a couch and pat the empty spot beside them. Her name may have been Angela, but she was no angel.

She sipped the drink and I put on my getting-down-to-business voice. "This whole thing is getting too complicated for me and you to play games anymore."

"How do you mean?" She still fenced with me, looking into me from those still, green eyes.

"Murray had been belted in the head. It may even be a murder."

She took another rapid sip of her drink, a longer one this time.

"Derek said it might get rough."

38

"Is that why he didn't take you with him, when he went in the boat?"

She lowered her glass, and her eyes, staring down into the glass as if all the answers were inside. Maybe they were, for her. "He told me not to say anything to anybody."

I stood up, straddling a little, acting red necked and tough. "I'm not *anybody*. I'm the law enforcement officer of this area and somebody's dead and I want to know why."

I saw her cheeks pucker as she tightened her mouth. Then she shook her head, decisively.

"Is he in some kind of trouble? Why did he hire a security man?"

She set down the glass. "He said to say nothing."

I tried another tack. I sat down on the edge of the bed and took off my hat. "Right this minute, my assistant is calling Bonded Security. They'll tell me what their guy was up to, so I'll have most of the story. I only want you to fill in a few details. Is that too much to ask?" She said nothing and I dug into my memory, back to the lecture they gave me once on Parris Island. Me and a hundred other shave-headed recruits, as a change from marching up and down in that goddamn sand. "There's a thing you should know about information," I said. She looked up at that. "The trick is, you tell people only what they need to know. Okay?"

She said, "You sound more like a soldier than a policeman."

"I've been both." She looked through me again. It was as if her eyes were turned off, like a TV set, cold and empty. I went on. "Right now I need to know what your friend is doing up here. And why he needs a baby-sitter with a gun. And why the baby-sitter is dead, with his head laid open."

"I don't know," she said, barely moving her lips.

"Is Pardoe some kind of big shot?"

"Big shot?" She laughed. "If only you knew."

"Try me."

The drink had worked a little. She turned her head to one side, a sudden flirtatious flick of long gold hair. Her voice was alive again. "Are you a chemist?"

I nodded. "Sure. See the shoulder flash, p-o-l-i-c-e spells chemist, right?"

That stopped her. She shook her head. "Sorry, I wasn't trying to be cute. So many of our friends are chemists."

"Not me."

She sat up very straight on the bed, tracing the pattern of the spread with her little finger. I noticed it was free of polish, short and unbitten. She was not neurotic about her hands anyway. She said, almost to herself, "He's a good chemist. He should be doing pure research but the money dried up." I just listened. Maybe now she was going to spill something useful, not just what Superman did for a living.

"Where does he work?" I tried.

"Straiton Chemicals, in New York."

They were the people who were getting their recruiters kicked off campuses in the sixties. They were making the napalm that the cavalry bailed me out with at least once. I felt less resentful than the average arts graduate who had never seen a shot fired in anger. "They make weapons," I said.

She flipped her hands impatiently. "Among a thousand or so other things, yes."

Gunpowder or face powder, it was all the same to her. She probably knew them both by their full chemical names.

"How long has he worked there?"

"Around four years."

"And what's his title, his position?"

"Research chemist." Either the scotch had loosened her up or she was on an information jag. I quietly thanked whichever spirit was responsible.

"I guess I don't understand. You said he should be doing pure research."

She snorted, not looking up, and traced one square on the

40

spread with her nail, digging in so deep the line stayed, even when she was finished. "At Straiton you work in an area about this big. They don't want pure research, they want practical research." She made "practical" sound like a four-letter word.

"Cheaper methods, better techniques?"

She looked up, half surprised. "Exactly. Not knowledge for knowledge's sake, knowledge for the sake of the dollar."

"And Doctor Pardoe was up here because he was frustrated in his work?" I assumed that he would be a doctor; it seemed I was right, she accepted the title without batting an eye.

"Kind of," she said.

"And Charles Murray was along because Doctor Pardoe had found something important."

"Very important." She stood up and looked at me as if she were trying to guess my weight. Then she flipped up the mattress and took out an envelope, a flat manila envelope about half the size of an ordinary sheet of paper. I looked at her in amazement. She may have been bright as a star in her own field, but she was a babe in the woods at hiding things. It would have taken a professional literally two seconds to find something under the mattress.

She handed the envelope to me. It had no address but was stamped with the letterhead of the Straiton Company.

She said, "I may be wrong, but I have a feeling I can trust you."

I skipped any wisecracks. "Yes," I said. I tapped the envelope with one finger. It was rigid, as if something firmer than sheets of paper were in there.

I took out my notebook in its leather binder. Between the backing and the pages that logged the repetitiveness of my days at Murphy's Harbour I had a couple of property tags. I took one out and wrote her name on the top, then "One manila envelope, sealed" on it, signed it, and handed her the duplicate.

She looked at me, mystified. "Is this necessary?"

"It's your insurance," I told her.

She folded the slip and I made a motion to fold the envelope, not following through, which was fortunate because she stopped me instantly. "It has to be kept flat. That's vital."

"Okay." I opened two buttons on my shirt and tucked the envelope inside. "Fair enough?"

She nodded.

"Now, I'd like to phone Straiton Chemicals and find out who they have on staff who lives up here in the summer," I told her.

She stiffened. "Don't do that," she said.

"What would you propose instead?"

She wrung her hands. Only once in my whole life had I seen anyone else do that. It was a Jewish factory owner, the night his plant burned down. I had always thought it was an affectation, until now. "Please," she begged, dragging the syllable out to four times its length. "Please don't. You may be putting someone into terrible danger."

I lost patience. "This is getting ridiculous. I've got one man dead, two more missing, and you're playing your damn silly games as if none of it mattered."

She pressed her hands together and calmed herself, letting all the tension leak out of her fingertips. It looked like a yoga trick. "I promise you that if I haven't heard from Doctor Pardoe by this afternoon, I'll tell you," she said.

I tried a little toughness. "What good will that be if he's in the water, bobbing down to the lock like Charlie Murray?"

She looked at me with horror widening her eyes, then she matched me, brutality for brutality. "Then it won't make a damn bit of difference, will it?" she said.

She had me. "Mazel tov," I said and walked out of the door.

I went to the motel's office and got myself a ride back down to Winslow's place, where my boat was tied. Ross still wasn't back, and Sissie Lowrie was busy selling hamburgers by herself. I let myself into the back room and telephoned Straiton Chemicals in New York. The only guy on duty was a scientist who acted snotty when I got through to him on the night line. He didn't have any information. He snapped at me in the way New Yorkers have. I hung up and called again, this time to the police in Manhattan. The desk man was just as snotty. It was a hot afternoon and I guessed the inhabitants of his island were cutting one another up. He had very little time to waste on an out-of-town policeman, even a chief. I bullied him a little and he finally put me through to the right precinct. They had one number for Straiton Chemicals, the home number of one of their executives, in case the office was found open at night. The phone rang twenty-seven times. I gave up and called my own office to see if any more cadavers had floated down to the dock. The office was empty. Murphy was at home where the extension phone rings when the office is vacant. His wife answered and told me that nothing more had happened.

That left me with nothing else to do but try the waterway. If Winslow and his passengers had gone far upstream they must have passed through the narrows. Assuming that the others had not drowned, they must have come to ground there where the waterway narrows to forty yards. On one side is the mainland, on the other an island that reaches almost to the mainland the other way, leaving a gap of only twenty yards at one end. If they had drowned, their bodies would be there, in the cattails.

I started the motor and tooled off upstream toward the narrows. There were no cottages on the island. It was all swamp, a few drowned trees and a few cedars and the occasional rock. Other than that, it was a desert island, soggy and useless. I headed for the navigable gap between the island and the west shore, not sure what I was looking for but prepared to swat mosquitoes and cruise the reed beds, looking for the floaters.

I was close enough to congratulate myself on having an orderly mind when I saw the flash. It was almost an accident, a sudden pinprick of light. I blinked and slowed the motor, turning toward it. It was halfway along the island, on the downstream side. I grinned. This was it. The other two guys had gone to shore for some reason and been stranded when the boat floated away. I eased the motor up a little and nosed in toward the nearest rock.

I thought the men would be there, Ross Winslow, burly and foul mouthed, and the mysterious Pardoe, citified and elegant, face swollen up with mosquito bites, shouldering one another aside in their rush to get into the boat. They didn't appear. But I knew I had seen that flashing.

The hair on the back of my neck began to prickle, the way it used to on night patrol in Nam. I wished Sam was here to bound ashore and prod through the debris of drowned trees to find them. But he was back at the funeral parlor with Murphy.

I cupped my hands and shouted, "Hello!"

The sound died away, soaked up in the bush.

The mosquitoes found me and I fanned my face a couple of times and shouted again, quieter this time, feeling foolish. There was a pause of about thirty seconds, filled with the viciousness of the mosquitoes humming and the slack-string grumphing of a bullfrog. Then I heard the voice. Quiet, weak, it called out, "Help me," very faintly.

I climbed over the prow of the boat and tied the bowline to a root. "Keep calling and I'll find you."

The same voice called "Over here," faint and weak again. I swore once and then plunged ahead through the five-foot-high tangle of fallen trees and wild raspberry canes. The mosquitoes filled my eyes and ears with their noise and their joyful biting at my bare face. My feet sank ankle deep in the rich sedimentary mud, black and stinking. Swearing out loud now, I kept on, toward the place the voice had come from. This had better be important, not some fool with a bent for practical jokes.

Ahead of me was the last obstacle, a toppled tree, covered with green mossy slime. I pulled myself over it, crusting my uniform with green filth. I was angry. This didn't make sense, none of it.

There was nobody behind the tree, but there was a trail, broken canes and boot marks drying on the boles of other fallen trees, leading away to my right. I scrambled back on the tree and looked around. Nothing moved. And then behind me I heard the burble of an outboard motor. *My* goddamn outboard motor.

I dived back the way I had come, tearing through the growth as fast as I could move, but I was too late. I reached the shore in time to see my boat fifty feet offshore, its stern deep in the water as some unseen person sitting low in the boat cranked the outboard up to full speed.

My hand dropped to my gun. I drew it and aimed with both hands, but as I did so I saw a sailboat tacking down the channel, out where my bullet would end up if I missed.

The realization stopped me cold. I was no killer. I let the gun sink back into the leather and strained my eyes to see if I could make out the person in the boat. He didn't raise his head until he was a hundred yards out, too far for me to be sure whether his hair was gray or blond.

I swore again in a low savage monologue, taking time out to swat the mosquitoes away from my face. As I watched, the boat made a long left turn and headed north, through the narrows. That drove even the mosquitoes out of my thoughts. If Ross Winslow was in the boat, it figured he would have headed down to his place. The man there had to be Pardoe. It had to be.

45

It took me about twenty minutes to attract the attention of the people in the sailboat, and then another ten for them to come up close enough for me to jump aboard. They were startled. You don't expect stinking chiefs of police to come out of the undergrowth in mid-channel islands. I spun them a story about having been put ashore to look for a missing kid and my relief being late. They probably didn't believe me, but at least it saved the embarrassment of telling them the truth. I sure didn't want that getting around the district.

In midlake I managed to transfer to another boat, a power boat that dropped me at the dock of my house. The girl who was driving it was a dumb, big-busted blonde who snapped gum all the time and kept looking at me and sniggering. I sat there grinning like a stupefied saint and watching how the wonders of her front stretched her T-shirt and made nonsense out of the words on it. "Lone Pine Lodge" became "one Pin odg" under the torture. I thanked her and went into the house to change into clean clothes.

The mirror had funny news for me. The bug bites around my eyes and under my chin had puffed up. I looked like an overweight Rod Steiger who'd just gone three rounds with Ali.

When I took off my shirt the envelope that Angela Masters had given me was stuck to my skin with sweat. I pulled it away and looked at it carefully. This was the key. I stood there for a moment, debating whether to open it up. But I didn't. Rules are rules. It had been handed to me sealed. I would let it stay that way until I visited her again in a little while. After that, if there was no help from her, I'd open it up and see if it gave me any answers. I put on my last clean shirt and spare pair of pants, pushing the envelope back inside my shirt.

Then I called Murphy at the station to tell him about the missing boat. He wanted to know if I thought Ross Winslow had taken it, and I told him I didn't know. I told him to call the locks at both ends of our stretch of water and tell them to keep a lookout for the boat. He had the license number with him at the office. If the boat turned up they were to keep the lock half full, playing dumb while I came up there and arrested the guy in it. Times like this I wished I had at least one other fit man to help me. The City Department would have put a man at each lock and that would have been the end of that worry. For me it was yet another juggled ball in the air.

I bundled up my dirty clothes after calling Murphy and walked down to Main Street to leave them at the cleaners. He's a smiling old Chinese who likes me because I have a few words of Mandarin. As a favor he promised to have them ready for the morning. Then I picked up the car from the marina and went to the office. Murphy was typing. Sam was lying on the floor. He sat up when I came in and Murphy told him "Okay, Sam, go to Reid." He bounded over like a kid let out of school. I rolled him over and bumped his chest while he squirmed with delight. I wondered for the hundredth time whether it was possible to get that kind of loyalty from a human being.

After a moment I straightened up, hung up the car keys, and sat on the stool behind the counter. "This is a lot more complicated than it looks," I said. "This Pardoe has something big to discuss with somebody here. He brings up a bodyguard and the bodyguard gets himself killed. Pardoe goes missing, so does Ross Winslow, and so does the police boat. And we still don't know who Pardoe was trying to see or what he was here to see him about anyway."

Murphy shrugged. "Must be somebody who's up here on vacation; that's all I can think."

"Yeah, me too. So what we have to do is ring everyone at any of the lodges and see if they have any Americans staying with them, people from New York for openers."

"What if the guy's got a place of his own here?"

"You'd already know who he was," I said simply.

His grin dug quick trenches in his craggy old face. "You got a lot of faith in my memory. There must be fifty Americans got places here."

"Try 'em all," I said. "Anything else happen while I was out losing the boat?"

He thought a moment. "Oh yeah, that girl was in, the one from the funeral parlor."

I wondered why he hadn't told me first. "When?" was all I asked.

"Just after you phoned. Said you had some property of hers. I told her you hadn't left it here. She said she'd come back."

"Great," I said irritably. "Why didn't you ask her to hang on for me?"

Murphy looked wary. I don't often bite his head off, anybody's head for that matter. "I suggested that. She said she couldn't."

"Did she say anything else?"

He looked thoughtful, then shook his head. "Nothing else. But it was funny, ya know. She looked as if she'd been hit in the face."

4

I shouted. "Hit in the face? Why in hell didn't you tell me right away?"

"I just told you." He was shouting himself now. "You're s'posed to be the policeman. I'm just the goddamn mister, remember?"

I came down. His contempt at his own lack of rank was embarrassing. "Okay. I'm sorry I flipped. But it's important. It sounds like her boyfriend came back and slapped her around for giving me the envelope." I was pacing up and down in frustration. Sam watched me, chin on the floor, eyes following my spitshined boots.

Murphy was calm again. This was the first time I'd ever seen him angry. "What envelope?"

I patted my chest. "The one she gave me to keep for her." He started to speak but I cut him off with a thought of my own. "Was there anyone with her?"

He shook his head. "No. I checked. She came in that Volvo of hers and she left on her own, drove back out of town to the highway."

"Back to her motel. Get the car keys, I'll go up there and talk to her."

He reached behind him and took the keys of the cruiser off the hook on the wall. He held them out, then held on to them as I reached. "Maybe you should put that envelope in the safe if it's that important."

"I'd feel safer hanging on to it," I said, taking the keys. "Whatever's inside has cost one guy his life and her a punch in the mouth. I'd like to keep it with me."

"You're the chief," he said reluctantly.

"Yeah. And I'm about to act like one." I took out the envelope and tore it open.

Inside there was a thin folder and inside that a flat black disk of plastic.

"What in hell is that?" Murphy wondered.

"Looks like a computer diskette," I told him. "It's got some computer data on it, I guess." I looked at its smooth blankness. "It's important enough to bring from New York under guard. And it doesn't mean a damn thing to anyone who hasn't got the right computer program to play it back."

Murphy said, "I figure it belongs in the safe, Reid."

"Later," I told him and whistled Sam. "I'm going up to the motel. If she comes back, ask her to wait."

I guessed she had checked out as soon as I pulled in and saw that her Volvo was gone. Oh sure, she might have been out somewhere, but the way things were moving she was covering her back and she'd be gone from here.

I opened the door and sent Sam in ahead of me to search. There was no way of knowing whether the mad doctor had a gun of his own and had staked the place out. He hadn't. Sam made a quick spin around and came back to me. I went in and checked. The birds had flown, sure enough. The suitcases and few hanging clothes were gone. The bed was still unmade, but

50

one thing had changed. The Cinzano ashtray was full of butts.

I'm no Sherlock Holmes, but that was evidence. Angela Masters didn't smoke. Somebody had been here, spent a little time. I checked the butts. Two brands, both American.

I pulled the door shut and went over to the office. There was nobody at the desk and I leaned on the bell. Still nothing. I figured that the boss was taking a tumble with the hired help. Jenny Saunders isn't much to look at, but neither is Mike and she didn't do much work in making up the cabins. I figured they were mom and popping out back.

As I waited I heard a wailing of horns out on the highway. I looked out and saw a snake of motorcycles threading down the white lines on the highway, passing everything. My gut tightened. It was the motorcycle gang from Toronto. If they knew I was here they'd feel obliged to hoorah the place, just to show how ballsy they were. And if I came outside they would fight. I found myself breathing shallow, tense as a bow string. I had a murder to look after, plus an abduction and a disappearing boat. This was not the day to get into a bloody hassle with some spaced-out speed freaks who would have a holiday in the newspapers if I took the gun to them, and would leave me for dead if I didn't.

My luck was running good that minute. They sailed on by, not looking sideways to see the cruiser in front of the cabin. If they remembered, they would be back, and the fight would be on.

I was turning to go when Mike Higgins came out, yawning to let me know he had been sleeping, not making out. He didn't have anything much to tell me. The room had been paid for with an envelope stuffed under the door of the office. It was an envelope from the drawer of the cabin and it had a U.S. twenty stuffed inside. Someone had written "Cabin Four" in sprawling letters on the envelope.

I left him, still yawning and scratching, willing me to leave so he could get back to his woman. I made my way back to the cruiser and drove down to Ferry Beach Lodge. It was time to take a real look around.

Sissie Lowrie was still working, and working on a bottle of rye that she covered with a towel when I came into the cafeteria. There were three or four teenagers in the place. They had cokes but weren't drinking them. When they saw me they left, pronto. I wondered just what Winslow's place was famous for. It sure wasn't the haute cuisine. I walked through the little lift-up flap to the back of the counter and took the towel off Sissie's rye. "Is this what Ross is selling the kids?"

She looked at me for perhaps half a minute, wondering if I'd go away. When she decided I wouldn't, she said, "I just work here, eh?"

"And you shouldn't be drinking."

She narrowed her eyes and worked her mouth a little. I guessed she was worried that I'd tell her husband and he'd give her hell for not bringing the bonanza home with her. "You ain't gonna make trouble, eh, Chief?"

I picked up the rye bottle. "You didn't answer my question. Is this what makes Ross so popular with the kids?"

She shook her head and sat down helplessly. "He never tells me nothing. I guess he lets the lodge guests have the odd bottle on the weekend."

"So what's with the punks hanging around here?"

Her eyes were on the bottle, like Moses staring at the Promised Land. "Why'nt you ask them?"

I set the bottle down again. Her sigh filled the muggy kitchen like steam. "I'm going to take a look around inside," I told her. Maybe she knew it was outside my rights. She didn't care. As long as the bottle stayed in the kitchen, so would she. She just nodded and I nodded back, polite as a couple of Mandarin dolls, then I went on through the back exit of the kitchen, into Ross Winslow's living quarters.

There were two rooms and a john.

The first room had a table and one chair, a couch, a TV set, and a dry sink with a couple of bottles on the top of it. They were rye, all the same brand, sealed from the liquor store. This was where he obliged his guests with a little weekend blind-piggery.

I checked the bottom half of the dry sink and found it locked. It was an unslippable lock, the dead-fall variety that needs to be forced, unless you had been in the Marines with a good ol' boy from Kentucky who shared his simple skills with you. It took me thirty seconds to open it and solve the riddle of the groupies in the coffee shop.

The sink had two old-fashioned cracker tins in it. One was filled with little plastic bags of marijuana, the other with pills. I took a few of them out and broke one open, tasting the bitterness on the tip of my tongue. Speed.

I dug farther down and came up with some sealed packs of white powder. I left them sealed but put them into my shirt pocket. I didn't think they would be heroin. The security was too casual. I assumed they were speed for the occasional freak who shot the stuff rather than dropping it. Of course, if I'd been doing things by the book I'd have picked up a search warrant, then I could have scooped the lot and seen Winslow slapped inside. This way the law was going to be rougher on me than it was on him. So I closed the cracker tins and the dry sink, relocked the dinky little lock, and went through to the bedroom.

Searching a room is a skill, like packing a suitcase. The pro makes it look easy. He checks all the places that people think he's never going to find, without disturbing the look of the place. I found that Winslow had more than seven hundred dollars in small bills, a collection of expensive pornography, most of it homosexual, and no gun or spare ammunition to indicate that he owned one.

The last thing I went through was his wardrobe. It consisted of a couple of pairs of check pants and a good windbreaker. There was one suit that looked as if it had last been worn when he came marching home from WW2. And there was a heavy jacket.

In the jacket I found the first thing that tied him into my mystery. It was a map of the area, an ordinance survey large-scale job. It was nothing special in itself. He had another one, identical to it, pinned on the wall of the coffee shop for the information of his guests. But what made this one special was a pencil mark, a small neat cross in mid-channel, upstream from the narrows.

I unfolded the map flat and checked references, not the figures but the lines of sight that crossed at that point on the waterway. It seemed that the point lay on a line between one small island and a prominent rock on the shoreline. That was the east–west axis. North–south it lay on a line between the mouth of the narrows and the mid-channel marker a mile upstream. I thought about it all for a minute. Then I folded the map and put it back in the jacket. It seemed to me that Winslow had picked out a rendezvous point in a remote part of the waterway. I wondered why. I wondered who he was planning to meet there and why he should choose a place that looked casual but was far away from any cottage or place where people might be watching. Perhaps it was the spot he had been heading for when his boat had been stopped by someone's cutting the fuel lines. It made the hairs on my neck tingle. It fitted. Winslow was tied in with drugs. That meant he could be involved with some heavyweight rounders. Perhaps they knew that Pardoe was coming to Murphy's Harbour. Perhaps they arranged to wait for him there, making sure that Winslow would bring him to them. Maybe they were the people that Pardoe was coming to visit.

I nodded to Mrs. Sissie and left. Sam was outside, ignoring

the vacationers who were making cootchy-coo noises at him. I whistled and he followed me back to the cruiser. I hit out for the office, excitedly forming my next plan. It was close to two o'clock and my gut started to remind me that I was there to keep it quiet. Murphy had gone home for lunch and the office was empty, so I phoned the restaurant to send me up a sandwich.

I'd just hung up when the screen door clattered. I looked up and saw a stranger, a big man with an old-fashioned fedora flat on his head. He was about forty, good build, sallow complexion, pale blue eyes, hair sandy, dusting to gray at the temples. I thought: copper!

He came up to the counter and took out a leather billfold that he swung open for me. It had a shield inside, Bonded Securities.

"Reid Bennett, Chief of Police," I said. "You here about Murray?"

"Yeah. The name's Fullwell, Simon Fullwell." He stood there as if he expected me to genuflect. I said nothing. He realized I wasn't impressed and tried a little bark. "You find the body?"

"No." He was annoying me. Security companies are a dime a dozen. Most of the guys in uniform are no-hopers, working for minimum wage at a job that requires nothing more complicated than staying awake all night. If he wanted to play detective, he would have to go by my rules.

He stood and looked at me again, stiff as a bird dog on point. Then he slowly unbent and leaned both hands on the counter. "Look, Chief. I've got a job to do. Okay? I also have an organization behind me. One of the things we do is keep records of every law enforcement agency in the area wo cover."

"Very professional," I said.

He nodded, acknowledging the politeness. "Yeah, so on my

way here I rang the office and checked on Murphy's Harbour. I found out that you're an ex-Toronto detective. You used to be in the U.S. Marines when you were in your hell-raising stage. You learned how to kill people." He paused and took off his hat, looking down into it briefly as if it contained the notes he needed. It didn't; there was nothing there but the smell of hair oil. He looked up again, laying the weight of his tired flat eyes on me. "So a year ago you had a little trouble with three bikies. You took two of them out for keeps, put the other one in hospital for months."

"You keep good records," I said.

He nodded again. "Yeah. And you're not a dumb hick of a country copper. So I'd appreciate any help you can give me. A guy of mine got himself dead on your turf and I have to find out why. You understand."

"I've got one corpse, two missing men, a 'now you see her now you don't' blonde, and I'm not any further ahead than you," I told him. I was starting to relax about him; he was off his own patch and needed help. As long as he didn't intend to sit on his high horse, I'd do what I could to help him. He took his hat off again and tossed it on the counter. It was a peace offering, the kind of submission one dog makes to another when he knows he can't win.

He stood staring at his hat while he patted his pockets until he came up with a little tin of Dutch cigarillos. He offered one to me but I shook my head. He lit one and relaxed some more. "Can't you afford an air conditioner? It's gotta be ninety in here."

"Low budget," I said and we both grinned. "Look," I said, "here's what I've got. Murray was retained by a guy called Pardoe. The pair of them, along with Pardoe's girl friend, blonde called Angela Masters, came up here last night. The guys got in a boat with a local lodgekeeper and took off up-channel. The girl took a motel room. The boat was found after midnight, floating with its fuel lines cut. This morning, the body of Murray, still carrying his .38, was washed up at the lock. The other two guys are still missing."

He spat a shred of tobacco off his tongue. "Great," he snorted. "You figure they drowned?"

I told him the rest of what I knew, including the stolen boat. He didn't grin, so I knew it was as heavy as I was starting to believe. "Okay, your turn. What do you know about Pardoe?"

He reached in his pocket and took out a notebook similar to my own. "We don't have anything on the computer about him, but we do have a good contact in the personnel office of Straiton . . ." He paused and read from his notes. "Pardoe. He's British, a scientist employed in research at Straiton. Salary eighty-five thousand, so I guess he's a heavy. He got his first two degrees in England, took his doctorate in California, working on the effects of . . ." He looked up, frowning in disgust. "My writing's godawful. What the hell is it?" I waited. He snapped his fingers as if that might decode the hen tracks. "You know . . ."

"Not if it's chemical. The only scientific words I know are coitus interruptus and aspirin."

He skated by that one. "No, not that. I remember, steroids."

"Drugs!" I said. "Here. Take a look at what I turned up in the lodge where the missing boat owner lives." I showed him the packages I'd removed from Winslow's dry sink. Fullwell bent his head over them for a moment. "This thing is starting to hang together," he said quietly.

5

My sandwich arrived and we split it while we tried to kick some more sense out of the few facts we had. Fullwell had a description of Angela Masters, from his source at Straiton. "Seems she's a chemist, twenty-eight, kind of a looker. She's been at Straiton since college and has a reputation for keeping company with the top-echelon people."

"Kind of a corporate groupie?" I suggested.

Fullwell snorted. "I wouldn't go that far, but it seems she hangs around with whoever the rising star is. The last six or eight months, it's been Pardoe."

"Lucky guy," I said.

Fullwell shook his head. "Seems she busted up his marriage, not that it was any hell before, he'd been separated, but the wife came into the office and made a fuss."

"You think that's why they hired your guy?"

He shook his head again. "This was bigger than that. You don't hire an armed guy unless you've got something that needs special protection."

"And unless other people might know where you're headed with it." I thought out loud. "Tell me, can this contact of yours check there and see if anyone at Straiton has a cottage up here?"

"I can try. But it's Saturday, and this person may not be free to go into the office on a weekend. He likes to keep his snooping down to office hours, he doesn't want anyone to know he's in cahoots with us. Listen, I'll call my people in New York, get them on it for me." He picked up the phone and called his New York head office, using his credit card.

I listened while he caught an earful from the guy on the other end. He stuck it out, then gave his instructions, quickly and clearly. "I know damn well it's Saturday afternoon. I oughta be out in the sunshine too, but those are the breaks, and it's your man who's dead, so get off your butt and find out what I need to know." He hung up with a clatter and sat looking at the phone with hatred in his eyes. "New York. They still think they're the world and the rest of us are outer space."

"Murray is one of theirs," I reminded him. "They're uptight."

"Yeah. Me too." He stood up. "I should go take a look at the body, make sure it's Murray. They sent me a wire picture of him. That's all I've got to go on."

He showed me the picture and I checked. "That's our stiff."

"It figures," he said, "but for the book, I'll go check. What are you gonna do?"

I hadn't told him quite everything. I didn't think he needed to know about that cross on the map. That was just a hunch, no sense two grown men following up a will-o'-the-wisp.

"The guy who took my boat headed north. I'm going to take a look up there and see if I can find it. It ain't clever, but it could be productive."

"Who's gonna mind the store?"

"Murphy, our mister."

He grinned in amusement. "You mean you're it? The whole department, under that hat?"

"Don't discount Sam," I said, and the big dog looked up and waited for an order. I told him "easy."

"How about this mister?" Fullwell was being professional; he wanted the facts. "Is he dependable?"

"As a rock. He's been in this office since he came back from the war. It he hadn't gotten himself shot up, he'd have been a wheel in this town. His father owned most of the shoreline, up until the Depression, when the bank got it. But the locals respect Murphy, he's one of their own."

Fullwell strolled to the exit in the counter, swinging his legs the way patrol car coppers do after hours in the driver's seat. "So how do I reach you again?"

"I'll come back here later, say around six. We can compare notes then."

He nodded and flicked the brim of his hat with one finger, the way they used to do in westerns. I could hardly keep from laughing.

I phoned Murphy at home. His wife told me he was spraying his roses and I told her to wish him luck. If I needed him I'd give him a call later. A man deserved a lunch break, and if Murph went to an hour and a half, well, he made up for it with his twenty-four-hour care of the telephone and his long hours at the office when he was needed. At the moment I didn't see what else he could do. I assumed he'd already tried to find out if anyone from New York was staying locally. If he had any information for me, he'd have passed it along. I whistled Sam and left, locked the office, then drove down to the marina.

George, the Indian kid, was sitting in the sun in front of the gas pump. He had a book in front of him but wasn't reading. He was watching a blonde in a bikini sunning herself on the deck of one of the tied-up cruisers. I didn't blame him. She had it all over *War and Peace* like a tent. He jumped up when I came down the dock. "Those big feet, Reid, you'll never sneak up on an Indian."

60

"Okay, Tonto. What can you show me in a power boat?"

He grinned. "I heard some dude made off with yours."

"He will live to regret it," I said.

The blonde heard us talking and raised herself on one elbow. Her top had come undone and we had a micro-flash of wonderland before she subsided again and fiddled with the string, writhing like a landed muskie. George sighed.

"It's about this boat," I reminded him.

"Oh yeah." He walked with me to one of the marina's rental boats. It was the same age as the police boat but with a smaller motor, for trolling. "Help yourself."

I got into it, calling Sam after me. He came and coiled down on the bottom, happy to be in the sunshine. I asked George, "Anything else going on I should know about?"

He thought a moment. "Nope. Except some guy on a cruiser must have had a birthday."

"Yeah, what happened?"

George scrunched his face, remembering. "Well, he tipped Crazy Eddy Crowfoot ten bucks for carrying a few bags of groceries down from the store about an hour ago, more, maybe."

I whistled. "He hasn't seen that much cash since they took the bounty off wolf tails."

"Yeah, well he's up in the beverage room spending it and he went to the liquor store first," George said. "More work for you later." He was right, I thought. Eddie made an ugly drunk.

"Which cruiser was it?"

"The *Mary Sue*, big job, sleeps six. Out of Honey Harbour."

I stored the name in my noggin. "Thanks, keep me posted."

He waved and sloped back to the gas pump to get his old view of the blonde who seemed to be doing isometric exercises designed to pop his eyes out. I backed the boat out from the dock and started away upstream.

I felt frustrated and a little foolish, following up nothing more solid than a hunch, backed up by the direction my boat had taken and a dim pencil cross on an old map. My mind was racing through all the things that might be done. I could be checking cottages to find if anyone knew of a connection between Murphy's Harbour and a chemical company five hundred miles away. Most police work is like that. You ask the same question a hundred times until someone gives you an inch, then you take in a mile of information. As it was, I was following a will-o'-the-wisp. But it was a fine blue-skyed day and the breeze of driving through the still warm air was cool and pleasant. I did what Confucius recommends in such cases, sat back and let it happen to me for a while.

Just through the narrows there was a boat tied to the marker buoy, something you're not supposed to do. Two fishermen were in it, dangling minnows in the hope of pulling in one of our muskellunge. They had beer in the boat and did a quick shuffle with their tackle box when they realized who I was.

I pulled alongside, careful to stay away from their lines. "Hi, been here long?"

"No, just this minute tied up to the buoy," one of them lied quickly. "You wan' us to move?"

I shook my head. "I wondered if you've seen a cedar strip like this one going through the narrows, about two hours back." They both shook their heads and I pulled away without bothering to listen to their explanations. They were lying about the time they'd been tied to the buoy and would protect it by lying about everything else.

I went on farther to where the channel widened again. It would be best to check the west shore first. There were fewer cottages there, fewer places that a man could get out of a stolen boat, and have a road to walk away on, instead of fly-filled bush. I could check it quickly, touch base with the lockkeeper at the other end, and come back down the east shore, probably no wiser than I was now. I figured this out loud and Sam looked at me, wondering if a command was coming. I told him "easy" and went back to scanning the horizon.

There were five boats in view. Two were sailboats. The others probably belonged to pickerel fishermen; they were drifting aimlessly down the current, their baits bumping along the tops of the reed bed where the lunkers lay, even in warm weather. I wondered if one of the hooks would grab into the flesh of one of the missing men from Winslow's boat. I kept close enough to the shoreline to look at all the cottage docks, but never lost sight of the drifting boats. I was level with the first one when Sam suddenly sat up and started sniffing the air.

I watched him. He doesn't spook easily and he's long since been taught to take no notice of some female in an accommodating state. His nose was high and he suddenly whined. I turned the boat in the direction he was sniffing. It was past the first and second boats, both of them with moms and pops in them, burning quietly in the heat. It seemed he was singling out the third boat.

It was still too far off to be clear to me, but it didn't appear to have anyone sitting in it. That's not remarkable. A lot of fishermen have a beer or two and then lie on the seat waiting for the big strike to happen to them. As I came closer I saw it was a cedar strip. And as I came closer still, Sam stood up and gave a short, urgent bark.

I wound up my motor and closed on the other boat. Even from forty yards it looked empty, but I drew my gun anyway, keeping my gun hand down out of sight in case there were only lovers in the boat, not my missing men.

From twenty yards I could see it was the police boat.

From ten I could see there was nobody lying on the seat. I slowed the motor but drove at the other one, hitting it a glancing blow that would have put anyone inside at a shocked disadvantage.

No head stuck up. No voice protested. And when I stood up, I knew why.

Ross Winslow was in the boat, lying on his back, dead, in a rusty mess of coagulated blood that sang with the wings of a million flies.

6

I put my gun away and silenced Sam with a word. Then, careful not to touch the interior or top of the police boat, I reached in for the bowline coiled on the front seat. I made it fast to my own boat and turned away, heading for the nearest place I could get help, the lock at the north end. As I drove I checked each way for landmarks. It seemed I was downstream about half a mile from the X spot on Winslow's map.

It took me seven minutes to reach the lock. My mind was racing ahead of the boat, working out what I would do when I got there. And I was going over the few facts I had. For one thing, there was no weapon in the police boat. It might be lying underneath Winslow, but it's common for a suicide to hang on to his weapon in his death throes, so it should have been in the boat somewhere if he'd done himself in. And secondly, the outboard motor was shut off and was turned the way it would have been to steer up against a dockside or the hull of another boat. It meant Winslow could have been alongside another boat when he died, maybe his marked rendezvous. It proved nothing, but it suggested that he had been helped to die.

I reached the lock and pulled in against the low concrete wall below it. There were a couple of kids fishing, lithe young ten year olds, brown as butterscotch. I didn't want them looking in the boat. I called Sam out and walked him around a circle about ten yards from the boat. "Keep," I told him and ran up the slope to the lock house.

The lockkeeper was a slow, fat man in his fifties, sucking on a can of beer some boater had given him. He saw me coming and tucked the beer behind him, breaking into the oily greeting of the mildly guilty. "Hi, officer, how's it goin'?"

"Where's the phone?"

"In the shack." He pointed awkwardly with his left hand, still concealing the beer with the other.

"Come with me," I told him and ducked into the shack.

I was already dialing when he came in. I spoke as I dialed. "Listen close. I want the lock closed for the day. Don't let anyone through, and try to remember anyone who's been through in the last two hours."

The phone was burring as he spluttered, "Don't let nobody through. How in hell can I do that? They're on their vacation."

"I've got a dead man in the boat and I need a tarp to cover him."

Murphy lifted the phone at the other end. His voice was calm, and it reminded me that I had to do the human thing first, before I got on with the police procedure. "Murph, this is Reid," I spoke slowly. Outside I could hear Sam giving tongue. Someone was going too close to the boat. Within moments they would be crowding me here. I covered the phone and told the fat man. "For Crissakes, put that beer down and get a tarp. Hurry, will you?" I spoke into the phone again, conscious that the fat man had not moved, would not move until he had heard who was dead. "I've got bad news, I've found Winslow."

"Dead?" His voice was without tone, dead as Winslow.

66

"I'm sorry."

Murphy cleared his throat. It was as much emotion as he ever showed. "Drowned?" he asked.

"I think he was murdered. His throat is cut and no weapon in sight. I'll know better when I've had a chance to examine the body."

There was a long silence on the line and Sam's barking outside, and then the shouting started.

I did what had to be done. "I'm closing off the lock this end. Nobody gets in or out without a slip we can issue. I want you to bring a pad from the office and a date stamp. Then drive up here with the boat trailer."

"All right. Anything else?" He was calm again. It was wartime once more for an old soldier.

"Yeah, phone Carl Simmons to come down to the station with his camera. And put this on the telex, ready . . ."

After another pause he said, "Fire away."

I took out my notebook and unflipped it to the entry I had made earlier in the day. Pardoe's name and address, plus the description I had jotted down and the license number of the Volvo. I read them off to Murphy, finishing in the same instant that the first of the boaters crashed in to the lock hut with the news. He was a small man in a summer shirt, shorts, and sandals. His face was white and he was breathless. He started to jabber at the fat man, then saw me and made a grab for my shirt.

"Off'cer, quick, there's a dead man in the boat."

I nodded. "I know. Just a minute."

The man leaned against the wall, looking as if he was going to throw up while at the other end of the phone line Murphy read back the description of Pardoe. I heard it through, then went over the instructions again. He said "Check" and I asked him, "One last thing, have you got the funeral parlor's number handy?" He had it in the office book of primary numbers.

He read it off and I scribbled it on the wall. "Thanks, Murph. See you soon."

I hung up and dialed the funeral parlor.

A somber voice said, "McKenney's, at your service."

I told him, "Chief Bennett. Is Mr. Fullwell still there, please?"

The voice lost its professional ring, became humanly excited. "Sure is, going over the same stuff you did."

"Great, can I speak to him, please?"

"Right away." The phone was laid down and I could hear the faint sugar of organ music over the wire for a moment. Then a clatter and Fullwell spoke: "Yes, Chief?"

"Hi. There's been another development. I've found the body of our second missing guy."

"Which one?"

I told him and added: "His throat was cut, professionally it looks to me."

"Where was he?"

"The police boat he stole. I'd say he was rendezvousing with another boat. I'm up at the north lock with him now."

Fullwell asked the obvious question. "Any chance of isolating the boat that was involved?"

"I figure to close the locks at both ends. We'll check every boat that comes through for bloodstains or obvious clues of any kind. Plus any boats going in get a slip stamped with something from the office, that way we know who was in here at the time of the killing."

There was a pause, then he asked, "Who's going to seal off this end while you investigate?"

"Any chance of your doing it?" It was unfair of me, but I needed help quick.

"I'll get down there right away. I'll explain I'm your deputy and give people a slip marked with my initials if they come in. Keep me posted, will you?"

68

"Count on it. Meantime, I've got Pardoe on the telex, wanted for questioning."

"Good. Maybe the sonofabitch did them both." He hung up in mid-thought.

I hung up and got a tarpaulin from the lockkeeper. Then I went back down to the boat. The crowd had already gathered. They were staying out of Sam's way, but there was a picnic table on the grass and they were clambering on one another's shoulders to get a look into the boat. The camera flashbulbs were going off like it was opening night at the theater. I went by them all and into the patroled area, pausing to stoop and pat Sam on the head and tell him he was a good dog. Without him the boat would have become a mass of useless fingerprints by now.

I unfolded the tarp and swung it over the body, shaking it a couple of times first to shoosh off the flies. I was glad to be rid of the vision of the blind, staring face and the ugly mouth of the wound, peeling back minute by minute in the ferocity of the sun. It reminded me of Viet Nam after an ambush and dead friends, lying like spoiled meat. My stomach heaved with the memory of times I had caused wounds as fatal.

I went past Sam, patting him again, and picked up the lock-keeper from the crowd where he stood bristling, angry that he hadn't been able to get through to look at Winslow. I asked him, "How many boats have come north, out of the basin, since one o'clock?"

People called out numbers like it was a bingo game. "Thirty." "Twenty." "Fifteen."

I told the lockkeeper, "Let's go inside."

He puffed after me up the slope, playing his scene to the hilt. "What about these people? I can't keep them all hanging around all day."

I ignored him till we were inside. He was puffing, pinker than ever. The others packed behind him to the door, a clutter of vacationers, guys and girls in shorts, one or two of them in swimsuits. I smiled at them like an idiot and shut the door. "I'm investigating a homicide," I reminded him. "Ross Winslow's dead with his throat cut. I figure homicide comes higher on the list than holidays."

He digested the thought for a moment, then said, "Shit" in a voice that showed he had finally gotten the message.

"So okay, how many boats have come up from the basin?"

He rubbed a few of his chins. "I don't have to keep records, you know."

"And you don't have to drink beer in a public place, either, so let's try to remember."

He looked blank. His head wasn't working. Maybe it never had worked worth a damn. He was some councilor's brother-in-law and the job had come to him because he happened to be there. I gave him a lead. "It takes what—five minutes—for the lock to fill?"

He nodded, slowly.

"So it's now—" I checked my watch—"two thirty. If you'd let six boats at a time through, that would be a maximum of fifteen times six; ninety boats."

He adjusted the figure for me. "No, it takes just as long to let a load down again."

"Okay, so you've let a maximum of fifty-four boats out."

He thought about it and nodded again. "Yeah, that sounds right."

Outside the shack Sam was barking like a metronome as he patroled. And the sunworshipers were jammed against the shack door as if we were the last lifeboat on the *Titanic*. They were talking, laughing, animated by the greatest excitement of their lifetime. I looked at them and felt the same sense of futility that every policeman fights when someone is killed. It's an event, a cause for celebration. I could have sold tickets at ten bucks a throw.

The fat man was looking out at them, licking lips made dry by fear and pressure. His armpits were seeping and the shack was filled with the smell of his fear.

I asked him, "Remember anyone excited, nervous?"

The heavy head shook.

"Anybody noisy? Or too quiet?"

He started to whine. "Come on. I see a coupla hundred boats a day this time o' year."

I leaned back against the wall. "It's gonna get a lot hotter in here," I said easily.

He got the message. I watched him as he frowned, mentally turning his eyes inside out to get the replay of his afternoon. "There was a big American boat, from Ohio. There was a woman on board, kind of drunk."

I nodded. It didn't sound like my boat, but at least his head was working again. He spluttered on, remembering all he could, including the yacht whose captain had handed him the beer. None of it made any sense to my idea of what had happened, but I noted down the things he thought were different. It gave me nothing. He was a dull man doing a repetitious job. He might possibly have remembered a nude; other than that, he never noticed a damn thing until somebody pointed it out to him. I thanked him and turned him loose while I phoned the marina and spoke to the boss, Walter Puckrin.

He was breathing hard with exertion. When I spoke he said, "You sure pick your times, Reid; I was just beaching a cruiser."

"That's why I'm calling, Walt. There's been a homicide. Must have been done by somebody in a boat. I want you to keep a check on anybody who takes a boat out of the lake. Like the cruiser—how long's it been at your place?"

"Since 'leven. The people had their lunch over at the hotel." He was unusual for a countryman. He gave his facts first before asking his questions. "Who got killed?"

I told him and said it might be a suicide, then cut off his run of questions. He promised to keep a good lookout for anything unusual going out of the lake. He also told me what I didn't want to hear. "There's gotta be a hundred places around this lake where a feller could take out his boat. How you gonna watch them all?"

It took me a minute to think of a way. I dialed information and got the number of a radio station in Toronto. Then I bargained with them to send their helicopter up to mind the store for me, keeping tabs on boats coming out of the lake until dark. In return, they were the only place I gave news to about the killing. I was lucky. There wasn't a rock concert or a ball game or an earthquake or any other entertainment going on, so they settled for murder and helping the police.

I was hanging up as Murphy came in, white faced. He looked as if he was on the edge. One touch of sympathy and he'd fall into a well of misery. I kept it business. "Thanks. Got the trailer?"

He nodded. "Where's the boat?"

"Down the end of the grass, there's a beaching ramp there."

"I'll back down," he said and limped out to the car.

I waited for him at the edge of the crowd as they flowed into a new shape around me, like flies looking for fresh meat. I smiled nice and blankly and ignored them, keeping them back out of the way of the trailer as Murphy backed down into the magic circle where Sam patroled, tirelessly barking and snarling. I untied the bowline from the boat I'd borrowed and towed the police boat to the beaching ramp. It was easier to wade in knee deep than screw around at the edge and take the risk of touching the inside of the boat, so I stepped in. The crowd cheered as if I'd scored a goal. We winched the bowline up and pulled the boat up on the trailer. Everybody wanted to be part of it. I saw Murphy stiffen when somebody said, "Why'n't he let me help? That old guy's a goddamn cripple."

He said nothing and we snugged up the rope that held the boat on. Then I went around to the driver's side. "Did you bring the date stamp from the station?"

"Right here." He reached down beside him and held it up, not looking at what he was doing.

"Can you take over checking the boats?" I should have been sterner. It sounded like I didn't trust him.

"If it doesn't take running, I can do it," he said savagely.

"Okay. I know it seems thin, but it's all we can do for now. I wouldn't want a boat to get through with bloodstains on it."

"And if one of them does have, do you think he'll come up when he sees a search? He'll get out some place else."

"I thought of that. I've got it covered. There's a helicopter coming up right now."

"You called the OPP?" He was alarmed. I guessed he could see his job evaporating in the whirling blades of the chopper.

"No, a radio station." I filled him in and he nodded, seeming relieved.

"All right. I'll take the car. You take Sam," I said.

Murphy climbed out and I gave him Sam, who dropped silent immediately and padded with him toward the lockhouse. I was worried about Murphy's head being able to take the shock of losing his old friend, but with Sam along I wasn't worried about his having any trouble, even if he did find the guy with the knife.

I drove up and away as quickly as I could. I knew it would jolt the boat and disturb the body slightly but I was afraid that the souvenir hunters would mess up the boat if I let them get a slow pass at it.

7

By the time I reached the station the radio helicopter was overhead. And I paid the price. There was a crowd around the station house as big as the one I'd just left at the lock. The roadway was packed with cars parked down both sides and the center of the road was jammed with young people, guys in muscle shirts, girls in next to nothing, all of them tuned to the blast of the radio station that was coming out of a dozen car speakers.

They didn't even notice that it was the police car. The beer was out and it seemed to me that at least one of the kids was stoned. But when I flicked the siren on, they parted quick enough and I drove up behind the station. The crowd came in after me, flashbulbs going off as if I had Jackie Onassis in the boat, not a stinking corpse. I stopped the car and went back to keep them off. They shouted and jostled until I stared them down, smiling the whole time so nobody would take offense and give me trouble.

When they were quiet I said, "Thanks. I am one and lo . . . you are many . . ." that got a roar. "And I've got a lot to do. I'd appreciate it if nobody comes close to the boat." Somebody called out, "Aw, why not?" in a groaning voice and the others laughed. I waited and then answered him.

"Because there's a dead man in there. I'm not sure if he's been murdered. But if somebody messes up one of the clues that I could find, then the guy who did it could get away. Will you help me?" They all cheered and roared and I knew I had them on my side—for five minutes.

I used the time well, ducking into the station for the things I would need. I was inside perhaps a minute but in that time the first wiseacre moved into action. I came out to find him trying to tug the tarp off the boat. A lot of people were hissing at him but nobody was stopping him. They were too eager to see what was inside.

I came out and took him by the wrist, smiling into his face like a big happy moon. Even the people within two yards didn't hear as I told him, "Touch anything else and I'll take you inside and kick you in the balls. Understand?" His face fell open and he backed off, nodding.

I dropped my stuff on the grass that grew alongside the station and waved everyone back another few feet. Then I started taking the tarp off and immediately a dozen of them sprang forward. I stopped and stared them down and they backed off. I realized it was going to be hopeless. Then I saw an adult back in the crowd, a small guy in a shiny suit, a real estate salesman from the office in town. I called him over.

The kids parted to let him through, jeering and pulling him the way four year olds tussle the birthday boy, letting you know how much they want to be part of the action by acting casual.

He had the dignity of a lifetime's selling something people don't have much call for. He ignored the kids, pushing through them the way he would have pushed through the bush. His face was sweating and the armpits of his suit were dark, but he was my man, down to his six-dollar shoes.

75

"Yes, Chief?" he said politely.

I took him by the shoulder and led him down the side of the station, past the end of the boat. I had to turn and evil eye the crowd to keep them back. They came to the end of their string and paused, waiting for me to relax. I leveled with Curtis. "Listen, Bill, I've got a dead man in that boat and no help."

"Yeah?" It was a delighted question. I'd just offered him a ticket to the horror show and he was eager.

"Yeah. It's Ross Winslow, and his throat's been cut. I need your help."

"Name it." He sounded like a TV copper.

"First off, I want that tarp off there. Then I want those kids kept back out of my way so nobody touches the boat."

"My time is yours," he said solemnly.

I clapped him on the back and went to the boat. The tarp was loosely covering the body. I rolled my end back, keeping an eye on Curtis. His face whitened, but he was steady. He rolled the other end away and I took my first real look at the body. From the amount of blood in the boat I guessed he'd died almost instantly. The front of his clothing was crusted with it, the whole bilge area of the boat was flooded with it. It had dried in the shallow places, but the deep portions in the bottom of the boat still held fluid blood, and flies.

I heard Curtis gulp a couple of times and told him, "Look away, Bill. You'll be fine." He nodded and turned away, dumbly, but he turned toward the kids in the roadway and held his ground. He was going to help me, and I was saved from the ceaseless arguing that I would have been into otherwise.

Curtis impressed the kids with his color. For the first time they realized that this wasn't a game, that death was unpleasant. They called out at him for a moment or two, then fell silent, standing around like visitors in church.

I went to my work. With my notebook in one hand I went

all around the boat, looking at everything that was in it. I could see no knife, but that didn't mean anything. Even if he had cut his own throat, which I didn't believe for a moment, he could have dropped the knife overboard in his last kicking. I made a note of everything: the position of the throttle, the tanks, the presence of blood splashes rather than smears, the way blood must have spurted, judging by the clear patches in the partial shelter of seats. Then I shushed the flies off and started a closer investigation of the body. At least, I was going to start when I heard the cackling start at the back of the crowd behind me. I guessed that Carl Simmons was here.

Carl was the only identifiable gay in Murphy's Harbour. He was an elegant, tiny man in his middle thirties. The year-round regulars regarded him as kind of a pet. Most of them had only a vague idea about homosexuality and they couldn't really believe that this man with his pastel outfits and a lisp was anything more than a confirmed bachelor, perhaps a bit sissy. Over the five years he had lived at the Harbour, in his white cottage at the edge of town, he had become an institution.

I looked up and saw I was right. Carl was doing his strut for the young bloods in the crowd. He was dressed in pale pink slacks with a white safari shirt open halfway, revealing a heavy gold chain and his zodiac sign. I noticed automatically that he was a Pisces. He had his cameras dangling about him and was camping it up for the crowd, confident of his worth here and now defying any of them to insult him. They parted, jeering, and he came through, nodding graciously to Curtis, who turned to me for approval.

I called out, "Okay, Bill, I sent for Carl."

Curtis made a little ushering motion and Carl came by and up to the boat. He stood there for a moment, looking back at one kid who had been doing most of the catcalling. "Not now sweetie, I'm busy," he said and the kid went scarlet.

I stuck out my hand to him and he gripped it firmly. His voice became businesslike. "I heard it was a killing. I came as quickly as I could."

"It's a killing. Take a look."

He did, not flinching at the sight. "Poor old Ross, he doesn't look a bit well." He was working as he spoke, unslinging his cameras and setting one of them down. "What do you need?" he asked.

"In a word, everything," I told him. "I'd like you to shoot from every side so that I can get a clear indication of everything in the boat and its relationship to the body. Then I want some close-ups of the wound."

"Done," he said. He snapped a lens into his camera and went to one side of the boat. "How would it be if I went all around the boat, taking pictures every three or four feet?"

"I want overlap, so there won't be any blank spots if I have to check the shots over."

"Okay." He held up his camera and looked through it. "I'm going to need something to stand on."

"Stay there, I'll get a stepladder." There was one in the back of the station, in the little utility room where the furnace stood gathering dust until fall. I brought it out and he accepted it without comment. He set it up and started shooting, wrapped up completely in what he was doing. I stood back, grateful for his professionalism, and waited for him to complete the job.

His camerawork gave my own eye a new objectivity. I studied the remains dispassionately. Winslow had died trying to stem the flow of blood. His right hand was clenched close to his throat, his left thrown back. That didn't necessarily mean he had been murdered. A lot of suicides change their mind when the blood starts, but he was lying half across the boat. I tried to construct the circumstances that might have made the body fall that way. One thought came to mind. It would have happened if he had been standing at the time and if whoever cut his throat had grabbed him, probably by the hair, holding the back of Winslow's head against his own chest, cut, and pushed Winslow away as the blood spurted. That would mark the killer as a professional. There would be no blood on the killer, or his boat if he was in one. It had all gone away from him, toward Winslow's front. If it had happened from another boat, the driver could have been away from the scene before Winslow knew what had happened to him.

I was glad that Murphy had Sam by his side. Sam could handle a knife or gun faster than any human could change his position. Murph was safe, even if there was a professional killer about.

I was just congratulating myself on being so bright when Schulz the Reeve arrived. He was the head man of the village, I guess, the real estate broker who was the elected head of the town council and was the closest thing I had to a boss. Schulz was a self-important little guy, a snappy dresser in a ten-years-outdated way, the kind of guy who makes out with waitresses when he goes to conventions. He would have liked it if I kissed his rear in public, but I found it tough to be more than ordinarily polite. He came up to the boat and looked in. "Haven't seen anything like that since Korea," he said.

"It must have killed him very quickly," I said. I wasn't there to listen to his war stories. He wouldn't have listened to mine.

"Murder?" He did a quick little thing with his eyes, the "Dragnet" investigator to the life.

"I can't tell, but it looks like it."

He spat thinly onto the withered grass. I could see it was getting to him. "Don't you know?"

"There's no weapon in sight, but he could have dropped it overboard after cutting his own throat. When Carl's finished I'll move the body out and check if it's underneath." He turned back and moved to lean on the side of the boat. I brushed his hands aside and he almost went on his nose. "Sorry, I don't want any more prints on the boat; it's gonna take me a couple of hours to print it now."

He looked annoyed for a moment, then realized that Carl was watching, through the viewfinder. He immediately became stern and officious for the newspaper picture. Carl obliged him. "Watch the birdie," he chirupped and clicked while the Reeve turned back to me, showing his good profile, the side opposite his thinning part.

Like most amateurs he had no idea how the investigation should go. But he had the moxie to cover his ignorance. "What have you done?" I told him about the bulletin on Pardoe, the man who had last been seen in Winslow's boat with him.

"This boat?"

I shook my head. "No, this is the police boat. Ross Winslow stole it this morning while I was ashore searching for him and Pardoe."

That really gave him his opening. He swung a great verbal roundhouse, like a bar bully picking on a little guy. "You mean a respected citizen of this municipality stole the police boat and took it away somewhere and got his throat cut."

"Right on."

He snorted and stamped his foot a couple of times like a horse learning to count. "You mean that we have to believe that you are not responsible, that despite the fact that you were looking for him in this boat and that his body ends up in this boat, you had nothing to do with it."

"You think I did this?" I indicated Winslow's gaping throat, the open staring eyes.

"You have a certain reputation," he said, not looking at me. I didn't want to argue. The familiar sickness was rising in my throat. I didn't want blame, I wanted peace and quiet far from this kind of savagery, and here was this little Caesar taking cheap shots.

"If you were in Korea you've done your own share," I tried.

He drew himself all the way up to five seven and shook his head. "Not me. I was in administration."

I grinned. "Bully for you. Now get off my back. I've got an investigation to run."

He stopped tramping his foot and looked up, embarrassed at giving away the secret of his war experience. I kept a straight face while he shifted his anger onto me. "I just have to tell you that nothing like this ever happened before you came to Murphy's Harbour."

"Then aren't you lucky to have a professional on hand when it did," I said.

He played his trump. "I think it would be better for all concerned if we had the OPP come in and take care of it."

"Once you do that, you're stuck with OPP protection full-time. You told me you couldn't afford it; that's why you hired me. So let me get on with my job, okay?"

He thought about it, looking for ways to salvage some glory from what was after all a grubby little murder. "I'll give you until tomorrow."

I said thanks to his retreating back and went on with my viewing of the body. Carl caught my eye and winked like a conspirator. And as I recognized the action I realized how thin I was spread. There was not enough manpower for the investigation. I should have swallowed my pride and asked the Reeve to let me call in a few volunteers, but I knew it wasn't possible. If I was going to keep on working here, I had to be the boss. Otherwise I was done. It was worrying. I was counting on the help of a cripple and a couple of well-meaning volunteers. On top of which I was beginning to feel that old disgust with death. This was not the reason I had come to

Murphy's Harbour. If I was honest with myself, I had come here to turn into an old man, or at least to get my head back to normal life again. I was through with death, if only death would let me go my way.

I watched as Carl changed cameras and rattled off some insurance shots. Beyond him the crowd was getting restless; this was boring. They wanted excitement. Nobody had ever told them that death is ultimately boring.

Carl finished shooting and came across to me, shaking out a menthol cigarette from a soft pack. As I lit it for him he accepted gratefully, ducking his head and brushing my hand like a woman. Someone in the crowd laughed. Carl said, "I got all the shots you asked for and a few more. El Reevie-poo looking important, of course, plus a few of the exterior of the boat, the number, and a few marks that looked as if they might mean something."

"Great. Now when can I have the prints?"

He frowned. "Suppertime, I guess. I'll have to keep the King family waiting for the last shots of their darling daughter as a putative virgin." He did a little thing with his tongue in his cheek. It was odd; his campiness was like rising dough. It expanded to fill every opportunity it could find. I guess it was his form of toughness. I thanked him and he left, strutting through the crowd like a duchess on her way to the headman.

I turned back to the body. All the preliminaries were over. It was time to start searching. With the tip of my pencil I reached over and lifted the flap of Winslow's mackinaw jacket. And what I saw made me give a quick little whistle, a cheep of satisfaction with my own reasoning. The dead man was wearing a gun.

8

It was a Luger. Thirty-five years before, Ross Winslow's young fingers had pried it out of the hands of some dead Nazi in Italy. And now it had failed him as it had failed the original owner. There was some kind of poetic justice in that, but my mind skipped by it as I went on with the puzzle that had been shaping since morning. Winslow had been wearing a gun. Therefore he had been primed for trouble before coming to the marina dock and sitting there waiting for Derek Pardoe and his bodyguard to come cruising up looking for a boat to rent. Somebody had known that Pardoe was heading for Murphy's Harbour. Somebody, the same somebody, had notified Winslow to be ready for him. And now the same somebody had drawn a knife across Winslow's life.

I stood and looked at the gun, acknowledging finally that Winslow had been murdered. No doubt about it. A man with the world's neatest killing device strapped to his chest does not cut his own throat. If he wants things to go away, he sucks on the barrel of his Luger.

Without examining the gun any closer I checked the slash

on Winslow's throat. Now that the wound had dried and the lips of it had started to gape, it was easy to see that there had been two distinct cuts. The first might have been made by Winslow; it reached from under the left ear down almost to the Adam's apple. But the second, which started almost exactly at the end of the other, would have been impossible for a right-handed man. To cut that high would have called for an insupportable raise to the right elbow. Besides, most suicides leave a first faint nick, a trial cut to see if they have the nerve to make the big one. Winslow had no such mark. No, he had been killed. And what's more, he had been killed by someone he trusted. Otherwise this old soldier would have been holding that Luger and the results would have been different.

To complete my diagnosis I lifted the front of his shirt away from his chest. The blood had matted it to the flesh for a few inches below the cut but then there was a clear spot where no blood had fallen. That looked to me as if someone had sliced Winslow and then held him erect for a few seconds until the blood had started spurting, then dropped him back into his boat, still clean because Winslow's blood was pumping away from him. I pushed my hat back and scratched my sweating head. I was surely dealing with people who knew how to kill.

I fought down the ugly swimming feeling that the realization brought me and cleared my mind of emotion, turning instead to checking the rest of the boat. I did the routine things. I scraped under his nails, finding flesh fragments that seemed to me to have come from his own face. I assumed that until he suckered me out of my boat he had been stuck on the same mosquito-infested shore where I had gotten covered with bites. But it's policy. There was a chance that the skin had come from the hands of his attacker, and if it had, and if the guy had a different blood group from Winslow's, it might narrow down our search by a few million suspects. I scraped up some blood samples as well and put them in the little bottles in my kit. There was no doubt it was his own blood, but it had to be done, for the same, long-odds reason. Finally I checked his boots. They were heavy work boots, clogged with black swamp mud, the same as my own boots had been. This was the man who had stolen my boat. And a hell of a lot of good it had done him, I thought grimly. The only thing about the boots that held me was some blood splashes on the worn leather. They were neat drip spots, not the spurting splashes that lay farther away from the body. They confirmed my earlier thought that someone had held him erect while his life drained away.

I noted everything in my book and stood thinking for a while. It was likely that his murderer had been standing higher than he was. That would account for the ease with which the throat had been attacked. He had been looking up, throat taut, the murderer had grabbed his hair, spun him around, done his knife trick, held him, and dropped him. I was looking for a cruiser. It was supposition, but it fit the findings and I had damn little else to go on.

I went into the station and called McKenney, listening to the piped organ music at the other end of the line. McKenney said he would send the hearse. That simplified things for me. He was there within minutes, coming himself instead of sending the syrupy young kid he usually sent to the farmhouses of the elderly. The guy was a ghoul, but what could you expect in his line of work. He had brought his joe boy with him. I wondered who was minding the store, changing the tapes of dreary organ music while the elderly relatives of an elderly farmer he had laid out in the chapel were doing their weeping and handshaking and eventually their talking about one another's families and crops. The young guy was cool, but McKenney was like a bird dog, his horrible false teeth almost chattering with excitement. "A murder, would you say, Chief?"

"Could be."

The kid spat on the grass beside the boat. I watched his throat work as he swallowed his bile. "Looks like murder to me," he said thickly.

"You can't tell, you can never tell," McKenney said, almost happily.

We lifted the body out. I was surprised at the strength in McKenney's arms and his carelessness of bloodstains. It occurred to me that his black suit must be wash-and-wear. They dropped the body on a stretcher and covered it with a sheet. The crowd had pushed as close as it could, almost past Curtis, who was still standing there, faithfully keeping them back. One of the teenagers giggled, but most of the others stood very still. One even took his hat off, but he made as if to wipe his forehead. Respect was not cool and these kids would be anything rather than involved.

When McKenney and his boy had everything strapped down, I told them, "Can you keep it like this until I get in there to check the body?"

The kid looked surprised but McKenney had learned enough to go along with me. "Trust me, Chief."

"I do," I told him.

The crowd moved back from the stretcher as McKenney and the kid wheeled it out. It was all right to laugh and scratch around death, but none of them wanted to get any of it on them. It was almost superstitious the way they hustled back. About a third of them took off in their cars to hang around McKenney's. They weren't bothered about the investigation; the body was what attracted them.

Out of the corner of my eye I saw the others start passing what looked a hell of a lot like a joint. But I had enough to do fingerprinting the boat, so I ignored them. I only wondered if they were Winslow's customers, and where their next supply would come from.

It took a while to get everything done. First I checked to be sure there was no knife lying under the place the body had been. Then I made sure I had enough blood samples. And after that I started fingerprinting the whole lousy boat. It was a long dull job and I knew that I'd pick up my own prints, Murphy's, possibly some from George, the kid at the marina, then Winslow's. And if there were any others after that, and if the person who had left them had a police record, and if I could pick up a clear print with enough points of similarity, all I would know is that this other person had touched the boat. It wouldn't convince a judge or a jury that he had killed Winslow.

But I did my job. And I found that somebody had carefully wiped the controls of the boat plus a lot of the other flat surfaces where there could have been prints. I wondered if it had been Winslow, when he finally got alongside the boat he was looking for. Had he wiped everything down so that he would be able to dump the police boat safely and hitch a ride back to the dock at his own place?

And how surprised had he been by what happened?

I went into the back of the station and washed my hands carefully, getting the blood out from under my fingernails. Then I sat down and thought for a few minutes. I needed intelligent, willing help to run an errand. The only person I could count on late on a Saturday evening was George at the marina. Murphy I needed for the phone. Fullwell was likely to be busy alongside me. George was a good choice, if he was still at the marina.

I phoned and Walter Puckrin called him in. The boy was excited, glad to do some driving for me. I told him to come by the station around six o'clock.

While I was still on the phone there was a great roar from the crowd outside and then the deep beating of the chopper blades overhead. For a second I almost panicked, remembering all the times the chopper had dropped in to take out shattered friends of mine from Nam. Then I remembered my pact with the media. It was the radio station chopper, here no doubt to tell me they'd had enough and were heading back to Toronto in time for an evening at some disco or other. I went out, in time to find a trendy looking guy of about my age, but with that smooth, monkey-faced youthfulness that lasts into the fifties and then shatters like a dropped mirror. He had a mike and a tape recorder and was chuntering away into it. I went over to him.

He said, "And now here's Chief Bennett, the police chief of Murphy's Harbour, a man who's no stranger to the tough side of police work. Formerly with the Metro police department, Chief Bennett has come up to the peace and quiet of this beautiful resort town where nothing ever happens, until today . . . tell us, Chief, what's happening."

He stuck his big ugly microphone at me and I obliged him. It was payment for the scouting they were supposed to have been doing for me all afternoon while I checked out the boat and the body. "I want to thank station CHRP for coming to our help in this way. We're not staffed for emergencies of this nature and the use of a helicopter made things much easier for us."

He wanted more. He wanted blood for his listeners, but I kept it cool, making the obvious official comments about sudden deaths, not homicides. It wasn't what he wanted, but if it got the crowd to go home, it would be fine by me.

He made a production out of telling me that only three boats had been lifted out of the lake that afternoon. He had the numbers of each, and the locations. None was a cruiser, and I had a feeling it was a cruiser we were looking for, but I thanked him and finally he went away, stepping low back to his chopper and up and away to the cheers of the crowd. I felt the way we used to back there in the saw grass. They were leaving, drawing the same pay, earning the same goddamn medals, but home free while we pushed on with the dirty business of war.

88

When he was gone, I called Curtis off his job of guarding the boat. He was standing where I'd asked him to. By now his suit was black under the arms with sweat, but he was hanging in. I took him back in the station and cracked out the other evidence bottle I had in the safe. It was cheap rye and he choked on it but drank it down like a survivor. Then I thanked him and he left, with real news to talk about round the supper table that night.

After he left, I called Toronto, the police office I worked out of when I was a detective downtown. They put me through and I was lucky enough to find my old partner in, questioning a witness in a lousy domestic stabbing, as he explained with some disgust.

I made the usual noises and he laughed and asked, "So what's happening up there? You just heading out fishing? Or are you doing a bed check on the local ladies tonight?"

"Both . . ." I let him laugh, then went on, "once I get this damn murder investigation sorted out."

There was a clatter at the other end and a minor uproar, then my old partner came back on the line. "Bastard's drunker'n a fiddler's bitch, now he wants to go get some more booze." He stopped and spoke words of caution to his witness, then asked, "What can I do for you, Reid?"

I told him. I needed someone to push my fingerprints through the computer team down at headquarters. It would be quicker than my doing it by going through the usual channels. And on top of that I wanted a check made by the attorney general's office.

He agreed at once. "I can't touch the blood and the scrapings, you'd be better sending them to the A.G.'s office yourself, but get your messenger to bring me in the fingerprints and I'll shove them through for you."

"Great. Thanks, Mike. Soon's this thing is over, maybe you can bring your young lad up for some fishing."

"That'd be great." His voice was almost wistful, then it

89

tailed off in disgust. "Goddamnit. Now he's thrown up." He hung up the phone, and I did too. The squalor at the other end reminded me of what I'd left behind when I quit the Metro force. It wasn't all bad, changing jobs.

I left, locked the station, and drove out through the crowds to Main Street. The shadows were starting to pull away from the buildings and there was purple in them, like the bloom on a ripe grape. It was a beautiful time of day, but somehow it didn't register that way after what had happened.

I went to the back door of McKenney's and let myself in. The young assistant was sitting in the preparation room, among the marble surfaces with a bottle of vodka open in front of him and a glass of pop in his hand. As I came in he was slopping more vodka into the glass. From the casual way he was doing it, I guessed he was on his third or fourth. I hoped no more bodies turned up that night. I'd have to bring them in myself at this rate.

He waved the bottle at me. "Hi, Chief. Can I show you something in a vodka and Seven-Up?"

That line amused him and he snorted about it as I replied, "No thank you, I'll kill a whole bottle later on. Right now I want to search Winslow's body."

He waved again, a big, drunken movement. "Help yourself." I unwrapped the straps from the stretcher and peeled back the cloth. The kid was behind me, his breath rattling in my ear. "Jesus God," he said softly. "What a way to die."

"There's worse ways. He was lucky."

The kid couldn't handle that. He went back to his chair and collapsed into it. "You reckon?" he asked.

I didn't tell him about some of the ways that buddies of mine had caught it. He couldn't have handled any more. As I stripped the sheet off completely, I told him, "Ross was unconscious in seconds, most likely, hardly felt a thing." The kid sipped his drink, and grew up, right there in the funeral parlor. He would be all right. I was glad of the change. Winslow's body was starting to stiffen, I might need help with him before my investigation was over. The kid would be okay now.

I opened the mackinaw jacket and looked at the gun. It was sitting in a loosely put-together holster that looked as if Winslow might have jury-rigged it himself some time. I had the boy bring me rubber gloves and I pulled them on, hating the obscene way they plucked at the hairs on my wrist. I pulled the Luger out of the holster and checked it. It didn't smell as if it had been fired. There was a clean, old-soldier's smell of gun oil in the barrel. And on the tip, against the sight, there was a tiny scraping of skin.

McKenney's boy was hanging behind me like a shadow. I got him to find a little jar for me to scrape the fragment of skin into. He asked, "You think Ross hit some guy with his gun?"

"It's the only reason there'd be skin on it, right?"

I was wondering if it was Murray's skin. Was this the weapon that had made that gash on his temple? I said to the kid, "Can you ask the boss to get me a tissue and blood sample from that body we brought in this morning, Charles Murray?"

He nodded, "I'll ask him, soon's as he's through supper." I had a sudden vision of McKenney, with his semicircular dentures, sitting in a house filled with day-old flowers, talking in a hushed voice over the pot roast.

I went back to checking the gun. I was right, it had not been fired. The barrel was clean and unpitted. The magazine was full but there was nothing up the spout. Winslow would have needed time to cock it before he went about killing anybody. Maybe that was why he had used his gun to pistol-whip somebody, perhaps Murray.

I fingerprinted the gun, the magazine, and each of the shells. Then I took Winslow's prints and made my own rough comparison with the prints from the gun. It looked to me as if he had done all the handling on his own, but it was something else to follow up.

I went through his pockets. There were only the things you'd expect to find. In the pants pockets there was a clasp knife that had cost three bucks at the bait store, a spare shear pin for an old outboard motor, a key ring with a 303 service bullet case on it along with four keys, some change, and a dirty handkerchief. And there was a wallet containing a driver's license and ownership papers, a membership card for the Canadian Legion, an Esso credit card, a few receipts from a hardware store in Sundridge, twenty-seven dollars cash. That was it.

I took off his shoes and socks and checked for money or papers. There was nothing there. I also flipped up the collar on his mackinaw to see if he had slit it and used it as a hiding place for some of the merchandise from under the dry sink at his lodge. Nothing. I guessed all his customers were cash and carry. I didn't strip the body. The doctor could do that. He might find something a policeman would miss.

The kid said, "The doctor phoned about an hour back, said that delivery is dragging on, he expects to be here around nine." I made grateful grunts. The kid couldn't resist adding, "He said what in hell's happening? Two murders in one day."

"He watches too much TV," I said. "This one could be a murder. Murray looked like an accidental death."

The boy looked at me, his eyes narrow. "How about the skin on Winslow's gun?"

"You don't mention that to anybody, okay? It could screw up the case if it got out too soon."

His eyes widened and he nodded. He was sober now. The bottle was out of sight, out of mind probably. All he had needed was someone to stiffen his spine for him. He would have made a good soldier.

McKenney came back, picking his horrible teeth with his

tongue. The kid told him what we needed and he went off to get it, happy to be doing something productive. By the time he came back with the samples, I was ready to go. I took his little jars and left.

Back at the station the telephone was ringing off the wall. Every time it started, Murphy's wife answered it at their house up the water and I was able to work without interruption. I labeled all the samples and the fingerprints and divided my exhibits into two bundles: one for Mike Delaney at 52 Division in Toronto, the other, containing all the blood and skin samples, for the attorney general's forensic laboratory.

I was just finishing up when the door opened and George came in. He had gone home across the lake and changed into good clothes—blue jeans of course, but a clean shirt and his fancy shoes, cowboy boots with the Cuban heel that made him six feet tall.

I grinned. "Pretty slick. Going to cut yourself a swath through the big city women, are you?"

He looked a little sheepish. But he fielded it. "Hell, I don't get too many business trips, Reid. Figured I might as well look like an executive."

"From the knees up, you're uptown. But the boots are a giveaway."

Now he laughed. "Hell, I'm trying to pass as a cowboy, you oughta know that." For some reason he trusted me. Ribbing from a stranger would have made him fighting mad. From me, it was a laugh.

I got serious, gave him the samples, and told him where he had to go and who he had to see. I gave him forty bucks, which was all the spare money I had. His eyes lit up. "Buy heap much firewater," he said cheerfully.

"For the car only," I wagged a finger at him. "For tonight you're an acting police officer. No drinking. You wanna hustle some lady, you do it on cokes."

He winked at me and left.

I stood up and uncrinked my back, then went out and got in the scout car. The locks closed at dusk, but nobody was going to get uptight if I closed them an hour early, not tonight. When I got to the north lock, Murphy was sitting in the shack, smoking one of his hand-rolled smokes. He looked beat. Sam was flat out on the floor, his chin on the ground, but his eyes moved every time anybody came in. When he caught a hint of me he straightened up and whined.

Murphy grinned. "Must be nice being wanted."

"You can't beat it." I waited politely while he told Sam to come with me. I could have hooked Sam away from anybody, he was my dog through and through, but it was good for his training to go through all the motions. When he came over I wrestled him a little, then cleared things up with the lockkeeper. "Either Murph or myself will be up in the morning. Until we get here, don't let anybody out without one of those entry slips signed by Murph, or by a Mr. Fullwell, the guy who's been working the south lock for us today."

The fat man grunted. "Don't make no sense to me, little bits of paper . . ."

I could have argued with him, but it would have done no good. He was lazy. He thought with his guts, and any more rules than he generally had to carry out meant less chance of the occasional free beer. "Trust me," I said. "Anybody going into the basin, you give them a slip and sign it. Anybody coming out has to show you one or wait for us."

Murphy broke in, his voice tired. "Don't forget, it could find the sonofabitch't killed Ross Winslow."

We said good night and Murphy and I walked out to the car. He got in and leaned back. "What did you find out?"

"For one thing, Ross was carrying a Luger and it had some skin and blood on the barrel, as if he'd clobbered somebody over the head."

Murphy turned and stared at me, very cold. "Are you saying he pistol-whipped that Murray who drowned?"

I concentrated on driving back out to the roadway behind the little park where the lock sat. "You know this job as well as me, Murph. I'm not paid to think, I'm paid to find out. I've sent the tissue sample off, with a matching chunk from Murray for them to check. We'll see what the forensic guys say."

Murphy spat out of the car window as if he wanted me to know that the story was too hard to swallow. "I've known Ross Winslow forty years and except for the war, I've never known him to get rough with anybody." His voice rose angrily as he remembered more. "I've never known him to get rough with any *thing*, for that matter. All the years I've known him, he's never even taken out a deer license."

I said nothing, just drove, letting the air wash through the car windows and cool him down. He snorted a time or two and settled down quietly. Then I asked him, "What did you see?" His anger boiled up again. "I saw how people pass the day when they're rich, that's what. I saw them lying around on expensive cruisers with expensive women, thin women in little bitty swimsuits and glasses of good booze in their hands. That's what I saw. And I saw them laughing at us donkeys trying to do our job of police work with a couple of guys and a dog and a cripple."

I let it all go. I could remember days when buddies of mine had been wasted. Everything else in the day made you angry. Especially officers and dumb orders. After a pause to let him know I had listened to everything, I said, "I guess Fullwell didn't find anything either. That means that whoever did it is still in the basin." Murphy thought about it. I could see him working to push the anger out of his mind to make room for the professionalism, the patterns that could put his buddy's killers behind bars.

"What makes you so sure it was people in a cruiser?"

I told him about the way the blood had spilled, the way the body had fallen. He listened and nodded. "I saw a guy get a piece of shrapnel in the throat one time, in Italy." There was a long pause as his memory creaked back and remembered all the details that had been unforgettably vivid that day, and been overlaid with a thousand others, just as unforgettable, between then and the time he arrived back in Murphy's Harbour with a tin leg and a pension that maybe kept him in tobacco if he rolled his own cigarettes.

I said, "I was thinking of picking up some burgers and taking them down to the station, along with you and Fullwell, check where we stand."

He shook his head. "Bert'll never hear of that. Come on to my place."

"You sure she won't mind? Two extra guys turning up at suppertime."

Murphy snorted a pleased little sound. One of the good things in his life was big, capable Bertha. "She wouldn't say a word if I brought the whole goddamn Indian Reserve home for supper."

"Well, it's sure better than the Chinaman's. If you're certain."

"Positive."

We drove through town, along the side of the water and out to the lock. Fullwell was sitting on a bollard, smoking one of his little brown cigarillos. He got up and came to the car. "Hi, what's next?" His face was flushed with sunlight, and he looked tired but healthier than he had when he arrived in the harbor six hours earlier.

"Supper at Murph's place—hop in," I told him.

He squeezed in. Murphy made room, lifting his tin leg up on to the transmission hump, out of the way.

I became aware of the smell of Fullwell's cologne. I grinned in the gathering dusk. The biggest use for cologne in these parts was as a replacement for booze on slow Sundays. Full-well dangled his right forearm out in the wind. He was uncomfortable at going to Murphy's house, and he sounded us out before accepting it.

"You sure this won't be any trouble . . . ?" he tried. Murphy said, "positive" again as if he had it rehearsed.

We all sat quiet like good boys until I reached Murphy's place. It was as neat as a pin with those goddamn corny roses spilling all over the trellis around the door. It looked like one of those jigsaw puzzles you used to get of English country gardens. Fullwell got out and spent a tactful moment or two sniffing the flowers while Murphy negotiated his stiff leg out of the car. Bertha Murphy came to the door as we all approached. She was big and cheerful, one of the people in the world who have certainties in her life. She was certain of Murphy, certain of the essential goodness of the people of Murphy's Harbour, certain that Christ was a member of the United Church. I liked her. If my own wife had been the same way she could have weathered the bad times we had when I hit those three slobs.

I put it all out of my mind and lived for the warm, blowsily comfortable minute.

Bertha said, "Hello, Reid. You've had a busy day." She bent and patted Sam who was happily cocking his leg on the rose bush. "You too," she said.

Murphy said, "This here is Mr. Fullwell, Bertha. He's an investigator from T'ronnah."

"We spoke on the phone," Bertha said, wiping her hands on her apron and then shaking Fullwell's. "Did you get your sandwich like you wanted?"

"Thanks, yeah."

We washed up in the tiny bathroom and came back into the kitchen where Bertha was setting out cold cuts and boiling water for tea.

Fullwell had the awkward politeness of a visitor from another culture. He wanted to talk about the case but carefully waited for me to start it, and I knew it was hopeless until supper was over.

Bertha chattered. All the callers had been neighbors. No one had called with any useful information. People who knew about Winslow's death had called, knowing that Bertha would be answering the police phone and would tell them whatever she knew. We listened politely and helped ourselves to sliced meat and salad. The kitchen chairs were sticky plastic and the sweat was running down the inside of my shirt by the time I'd finished eating. Fullwell was about two bites behind me. Murphy was down the track, but he could see what was needed.

"Listen, Bert. We've gotta get our heads together; d'ya think you could take over the phone again for a while?" He left it a moment or two before adding "please" in a pleading tone of voice.

Bertha was quite cheerful about it. "You men get on with it. There's plenty more tea in the pot." She beamed at us all and left.

Fullwell relaxed at once. "I didn't see a damn thing at my lock," he said. "Not a boat came through that could have been involved."

Murphy cleared his throat. "Me neither. I don't think it was any damn use at all, Reid, you ask me."

Fullwell glanced at him in surprise but said nothing.

"It's the closest we could come to sealing off the scene of the murder. I'm sorry we didn't catch anybody with blood on the boat, but at least we know that the boat that was involved is still in our reach of the waterway."

Murphy said, "Great." Fullwell sniffed.

The heat was getting to me. It had already been a long hot day and we were no closer to any answers. I was beginning to lose patience with Murphy, but I kept it in.

"Let me just lay out everything I know, in one straight line, okay?" The other two sat silent. Fullwell brought out his tin of little Dutch cigarillos, offered them to each of us, then lit up. I said, "Ross Winslow was pushing grass and he was pushing pills."

Murphy shot me a look. "How'd you get to say a thing like that?"

"I went through his room. He had enough speed to get the whole goddamn district flying, plus some grass." I waited a moment to see if either one of them would ask where I got the search warrant. They didn't. "What that means to me is that Winslow had some pretty sleazy dealings. Somewhere down the line he had to be tied in with some rounders."

Still no argument. I ploughed on. "I also found a map with a cross marked at the approximate place where I found the boat floating today. Now, if you add in the fact that he was wearing a gun when we found him and that his boots were covered with muck from the island up by the narrows, I start to put a picture together."

Fullwell took over, so excited he forgot to take the cigarillo out of his mouth. It wagged as he spoke. "It could be that he was going to meet some guys up where he ended up. So he puts on his gun and goes over to the marina and there he is, waiting, when Pardoe and Murray arrive."

"He was at the marina every Friday night, regular as clockwork—he always came into town to go to the beer parlor," Murphy objected. "He's never missed. He wouldn't even go to the Legion on a Friday."

"Exactly." That was the cue I had been looking for. "And he was there at eight o'clock, regular as clockwork. Only this time he was fiddling with a motor that was already running good."

Fullwell took his cigarillo out of his mouth. His eyes were bright and his voice had picked up speed. He was thinking as he spoke. "So it looks like he'd been set up to meet those two.

99

It's easy for me to believe that he was trying to take them up to the point marked on the map."

"That's what I make of it," I said. "Only somebody cut the lines on his boat, most likely up near the narrows, so he couldn't make his rendezvous."

Murphy was silent. It was his own personal statement on the case, anger and frustration tied together, a defense of Winslow's memory in the face of all the evidence we were fitting into place.

"It all makes sense," Fullwell said.

"Yeah, plus the fact that Murray had been hit in the head, and when I checked Winslow's gun he'd slugged somebody with it; there was skin and blood on the barrel."

Now Murphy burst out. "Pardoe could've done that. Winslow never slugged anybody."

"He was pushing speed," I reminded him. "I know the guy was your buddy, Murph, but you have to admit he was into a dirty business. He could've picked up a few dirty habits, in private."

Murphy stood up. "I'll go get some more water for the tea," he said angrily and stumped out.

Fullwell said, "I think this is the scenario. It all fits."

"It almost fits," I cautioned him. "We still haven't found Pardoe, and the girl has gone missing. If we could get a line on them we could tie up the whole case and go home and watch the late movie on TV."

Fullwell stretched slowly and deliberately and crushed out his cigarillo on the edge of his saucer. "We have got to find Pardoe," he said.

9

We both sat still for a moment, looking like Moses must have looked when the Lord laid the tablets on him. Then I said, "There's one thing we still have in the hole."

"What's that?" Fullwell stopped in the middle of lighting another cigarillo.

I reached into my sweaty shirt front and pulled out the envelope that Angela Masters had given me. "This is the key to whatever the hell Pardoe wants to talk about."

Murphy came back in with the kettle. He looked at the envelope and said, "Jeezuss! How come you're carrying that around, Reid? That belongs in the safe."

"I'll put it in there later on. Right now, I've got it and as far as we know, Pardoe wants it, so he or the girl is going to come looking for it."

Fullwell was the first to take that one up. "I hope you're right, Chief, because otherwise we have to wait for the OPP to come up with them in their car, and that could be a couple a' hundred miles from here."

"I'm not holding my breath. This is a holiday weekend and

101

the OPP are all out there waving cars through tieups, blowing their little whistles. They'll never find a car just because we're looking for it, unless it has an accident."

Fullwell clenched his teeth on his little cigar. He reminded me of Franklin Delano Roosevelt. "Well, if that's the case, and I figure it will be, I should get myself back to Toronto and start our own people looking for Pardoe and the girl."

It had to happen. Our help was shrinking. Once Fullwell had driven away and Murphy had turned in for the night, then the whole case would turn back on me and Sam, one man and his dog.

"If you can get some gunpowder under the American police, maybe we can come up with them. Meantime, I'm gonna keep looking around here," I said.

Fullwell nodded. "That's all we can do. But what're you gonna do with that envelope from the girl?"

"I'll put it in a safe place," was all I promised.

He stood up, reaching down to lean on the table and stare at me. "Make it good and safe."

"It will be."

He nodded, then thanked Murphy formally for supper and went out to thank Bertha. She responded with a little ripple of talk that lasted while Murphy said, "He's right, you know, Reid, that's the only goddamn thing we got. Hang on to it good."

I stood up and pushed the chair back, politely. "Listen, Murph, except for this thing, we're nowhere. Believe me, it's going in the safest place I know."

He looked at me with an intensity beyond words, then slowly nodded. "Good."

"Don't worry. Take the night off, see if you can relax, have a few beers. I'm gonna take Sam around town and settle the place down."

He stretched back in his chair, the weariness showing in

every line. "Forget the beers, but I'll be happy to lay back a spell."

I banged him on the shoulder. "Thanks for the supper. I'll drop Fullwell back at his car."

He nodded again and I went through to the little room where Bertha was operating the phone. It was a curious forward projection on the picture of the wartime woman helping her man. Everything in the room dated from the forties, from her marriage; only Bertha was older, in her mid-fifties now and slower than she had once been. But she still had the same efficiency that had made her the go-getter of Murphy's Harbour when she married Murph in 1946. I thanked her and she waved an "it was nothing" wave and went on chatting on the phone.

Fullwell looked at me expectantly and I led him out again, giving Sam the nod to follow us out of the house. We went out to the car and I let Sam into the back. He coiled down immediately, leaving Fullwell and me alone to discuss the case. Fullwell was drowsy from the unaccustomed sunshine of his afternoon. I took him back to the station, and he got into his car like a sleepwalker. Then he wound down the window and called across to me. "There's gotta be a tie between Pardoe and this place. Maybe it was one of his bosses, maybe there's a mob heavy staying up here, something. I'll get on it."

"It would sure help," I said.

He waved, casually, one copper to another, and drove off. When he had gone into the gathering dusk, I turned back and glanced through the screen into the rear seat. "Looks like me and you take care of things, old buddy." Sam looked up briefly and bumped his tail, then closed his eyes again.

I sat and thought for a while, then decided what had to be done next. I drove off, back down the road to my house. It was dark, of course, and I went into the kitchen, the logical place anyone would expect me to visit first. I switched on the light and opened the refrigerator. Inside there was the inevitable row of beer bottles and a half-empty can of dog meat. I took out the can and set it on the countertop. Then I went out to the dog run, making a little pantomime of walking slowly and rubbing my neck as if I were weary, just in case anyone should be tuned in from the shadows. Sam's dish was there. I picked it up. Then I went back into the house and drew the blinds in the kitchen. I had a roll of tape in the drawer and I used it to tape the envelope Angela Masters had given me to the underside of Sam's dish. After that I tipped the rest of the can of dog meat into the dish and carried it out to the dog run. Sam followed, wagging his tail at the unexpected promise of goodies in the dish.

I set it down inside the run and gave Sam his go-ahead. He got through the meat in his customary three swallows and I called him back to the scout car. I felt sure that nobody would suspect I'd put anything as important as the Straiton envelope on the flip side of a dog dish, and I felt just as sure that it would be perfectly safe there, especially when I came back and put Sam in there for the night.

He got back in his old spot on the rear seat and we drove to town. The parking lot at the tavern was full. I guessed that murder was a big drawing card. Saturday was always busy, but tonight was frantic. The noise of the band flooded the scout car even before I'd shut the engine off. I got out and called Sam after me.

We walked in through the back door, into the kitchens. The Chinaman on duty grinned at me and I grinned back, two functionaries showing professional courtesy. I went on by him, through the savage heat of the barbecue pit where he was flipping steaks for the big spenders out front, and on to the inside of the bar.

Frank the barman was running draught beer, his hands moving continuously in a choreography that never let up. As fast as he could fill them, the waiter was putting them on a tray and shoving them out into the crowd. He looked up and winked and gestured toward me with a glass. I shook my head. One would do nothing for the heat, and two would take the backbone right out of me.

I walked past him and stood at the edge of the tiny dance floor as the four-piece group did their best with the golden oldies from the forties. Clem, on trumpet, was pretty good. He was handling "Poor Butterfly" with the proper respect and I heard him out, my eyes checking all around the room for anything suspicious. There was nothing. Nobody too noisy or drunk, nobody strange. All of them had the correct amount of tan that meant they had been here for at least today with nothing else on their minds but getting brown.

When he finished I waved to him and went back out to continue checking my patch, my whole moribund patch.

The marina was locked up. Walt Puckrin's dog, a big snarly castrated shepherd, was on duty inside the boathouse, so that was safe. The few front doors on the street facing the marina were all closed up, except for the restaurant. I stuck my head inside but there was nothing happening except for a few kids ordering up the specialty of the place, hamburgers and shakes. They looked at me straight faced and I nodded and went on out again. The big thermometer on the dock was registering close to eighty and the mosquitoes were humming. I felt glad to be living here, not spending hard-earned city dollars to rent an overheated bedroom in town.

Everything was fine. And then I got wind of the trouble. A car came roaring by me in second gear. It was full of teenagers and they exploded out of it, leaving the doors hanging open, and piled into the beverage room of our other hostelry, the local's local.

I called Sam to heel and trotted over to the back door, again, entering through the kitchen. Nobody ever expects a policeman to come at him the same way as his order of chow mein. Sam was right behind me as I came through the swinging doors and found myself at the back of a crowd that was standing on chairs and jumping up to see what was happening in the middle of the room.

There was so much shouting going on that nobody would have heard me even if I'd been stupid enough to shout. Instead I said a quiet little thank you to my patron saint and told Sam to speak. At once his amiability dropped off him like a mask. He became a barking slavering monster, his lips curled back to expose fangs like daggers. The crowd parted like magic, admitting the pair of us to the main attraction, a fight.

Big Eddy Crowfoot was taking on two very pale-faced cottagers. He was reeling drunk but still light as a ballet dancer on his feet. In his right hand he had the neck of a broken whiskey bottle, the remains of the brown bag he had covered it with still hanging down around the ugly jagged edges. One of the cottagers was bleeding freely from a cut hand. He was clutching his wrist with his other hand, looking around him and swearing in a frightened voice. The other man was tougher, holding a chair out in front of him, facing Eddy, waiting for a chance to pin him once he jabbed.

Eddy was cursing them in a flat, uninterested voice, urging them to come on, come on. It was as routine as Chinese theater. A couple of waiters were hovering around the edges of the fight, shouting, for what that was worth, and standing by to pick up bodies if Eddy did his thing.

Slowly they all became aware of Sam and me. The waiters backed off and the two cottagers begged for help with their eyes as they circled. I told them, "You two stand still. Eddy, drop that bottle."

He turned and focused on me and his face lit up with delight. "Hey. It's the tough guy. Eh? Eh?" He waved his bottle at me. "C'mon, Killer."

I took no notice and he raised the volume. By now the

room was silent, except for him and Sam, still slavering and threatening, giving tongue like a whole pack of hounds.

I kept my own voice calm. "Drop it, Eddy."

He waved his bottle again. He was enjoying himself. A fight would not scare him. He would keep going without malice until one of us was in hospital. Fighting was fun. I had gotten to know why Indians used to call their menfolk "braves." "Come on, Killer," he said. And other voices were taking it up. "Hey! Killer! Hey! Come onnnnn Killer!!!" Eddy looked around, cunningly. He was among friends. He could take my face off with his bottle. It was okay.

He waved the bottle again and I lost my patience. I told Sam, "Fight!"

Sam stopped speaking. Silent as the Angel of Death he lunged forward and grabbed Eddy by the wrist of the hand holding the bottle.

Eddy dropped the bottle and in the same moment he wet himself in shock and fear.

I told him, "There, see what you've done now. You oughta be ashamed of yourself."

The crowd had stopped calling out. They shared his shock as he strained back, tugging his arm against the clenched jaws. Desperately he kicked out at Sam, and then screamed as Sam automatically increased the bone-crushing pressure on his arm. I took out my handcuffs and hit him shrewdly on the free wrist with the edge of the cuff. It opened and flipped around his wrist, clipping shut on his hand. Then I whistled once, shrill and loud. Instantly Sam released the other arm. I could see deep puncture marks in the skin, but there was no blood. I asked Eddy, "You gonna make trouble?"

"Not me, Chief, honest." He sounded like he meant it. The crowd was jamming closer, one or two of the bold ones were reaching out to pat Sam, but drawing back when he fixed his big eyes on them.

I led Eddy by the handcuff I had snapped on him, giving the

107

other two men a nod to follow me. They all came, quiet as mice, back to the space behind the bar where the empty beer cases were stacked eight deep. The barman hovered over us, anxious to get his word in. "Thanks, Reid, I musta phoned a dozen times, but the station line was busy."

"People calling in about Ross Winslow," I told him. I gave Eddy a gentle shove, sitting him down on a couple of low-set beer cases. "Relax," I told him. I opened my notebook and wrote "8:50 p.m. investigate disturbance, Murphy's Harbour Arms. Arrest Eddy Crowfoot, create disturbance." I took the names of the cottagers. One was a regular with a place at the Harbour, the one with the cut hand was a friend, up for the Great Canadian Weekend of helping to build the cottage extension.

I looked at his hand. It was nasty, a cluster of gashes that was going to need stitches and a month or so of healing. Compared with Winslow's throat it was nothing. "That needs care. Better get to the hospital, right away."

The man swore, bitterly. "Goddamn hotel. You come in for a glass o' beer an' you get half killed." He was bigger than he had looked in his fear, maybe five ten with a good build. He was in his late twenties and his voice had the burbling, oddly stressed phrasing of the Maritimes. He verified it for me with his next action. Without batting an eye he lashed out with his right foot and caught Eddy neatly on the kneecap.

I got angry. "Listen, you ugly bastard, you do that again and you're going in alongside him, understand?"

Eddy was ruefully rubbing his knee as if he were a total stranger to the affair. "Shit, that hurt," he told nobody in particular.

The Newfie was getting bolder by the moment. "You think that hurt, do you," he raged. Once again I was grateful for Sam. Without him it would be a tussle that I could not win without hurting the man, putting him in hospital. His normal reflexes were all jammed with anger. Pain would not deter him; I would have to incapacitate him. Instead I said to Sam "speak" and Sam snarled and raged in front of him until he shriveled in fear. He pulled back, falling over a beer case and backing away on his buttocks, his injured hand held aloft like a trophy.

"You want your other hand in pieces?" I asked him.

"Call 'im off." He was almost screaming with fear.

I told Sam "easy" and he relaxed, a show dog again with a handsome, silent head. I patted him and spoke to the uninjured cottager.

"Now I'm going to make a couple of assumptions, okay?" He stared at me. "I'm gonna assume that you're sober enough to take your buddy to the hospital at Sundridge. Does that sound reasonable?"

"Yeah." He nodded greedily. "Yeah, thanks."

"You're welcome. Get him out of here, and keep his mouth shut."

I stood back, stooping to pat Sam's head gratefully, as the two of them made their way through the side door and out to the parking lot.

I followed them thirty seconds later, in time to see their taillights pulling sedately out of the lot. It was barely dark.

I went back inside. I had to take Eddy to jail, for one thing, and for another it's always good policy to stamp out the ashes of a barroom fight. They tend to go underground and smoulder once the first big blaze has gone out.

The barman was at his beer tap, working a shade faster than his opposite number down at the hotel. Murphy's Harbour was a beer town in summertime. He paused to slide a couple of cool bulbous glasses in front of me. Now I was ready for beer. I thanked him and took that first wonderful bite out of one of them.

The barman kept pouring. He knew and I knew that I was

breaking the law. Policemen do not drink on duty. But this was my patch and I had a couple of bodies to account for and I'd just saved him from an expensive bar fight. We would waive the rules. Only I had to remind him. "How long did Eddy have that bottle with him?"

He shrugged, moving from the elbows up, not disturbing the rhythm of the glasses under the spout of the beer tap. "Hard to say."

"You have to watch out for that. It's illegal," I said, and we looked at one another and grinned.

"I didn't know he had a mickey," he said.

"Of course not," I soothed. "Otherwise you wouldn't have been selling him beer, would you?" We laughed and I finished my beer and set down the empty.

I felt like a phony, a show policeman. Arresting a drunk on a night when I should have been looking for Winslow's murderer was frivolous. It showed me only how small my worth had become since that night in Toronto. I was a doorman for this bar, not an investigator, a lackey, keeping the peace while Fullwell went off to the city to try and do my job for me.

I went and collected Eddy. He was sleeping the sleep of the justly hammered, sprawled across the cases of empties as if someone had caught him a solid right cross. I woke him with a nip between finger and thumb under his armpit and led him out and back down the street to my scout car, parked outside the tavern. I took the handcuffs off him and shoved him in the back, where he fell asleep again, snoring happily to himself. Sam came in the front, sitting tall on the passenger side, my assistant. As I drove I reached over and did the little thanking things, bumping his big back and rubbing him behind the ears. He rolled his head in puppyish delight. I had a sudden image of myself, old and lonely, sitting on a park bench somewhere with my dog, the only creature in the world that gave a damn if I opened my eyes in the morning. The thought made me laugh at myself. What I was suffering from wasn't loneliness, it was responsibility overload. I'd feel better when Winslow's killer was behind the doors of my neat little slammer.

I got to the station and drove around to the back door. I got out of the car and Sam came after me, flitting out like a dark ghost. He hit the floor and began to growl, uneasily, roaming up and down by the door as I stood there trying to get Eddy out of the back seat. I told Sam "easy," but he didn't obey completely. Instead of falling silent he whined with anxiety. I assumed it was the smell of Winslow's blood in the boat still parked behind the station, so I repeated myself, "Easy, Sam."

I got Eddy mobile, using another horse bite to open his eyes for him, and steered him up the step to the back door. He fell asleep again as I propped him there, and then he woke with a start as he began to slip when his knees buckled. I managed to lean against him while I opened the door and let him half fall inside.

The first cell was open and I swung him inside it, flopping him out on the bare cement. Sam was whining again in a fury and I looked around to check that nobody was inside. I could see nothing, but Sam's actions worried me. I quickly slipped Eddy's belt off and then his bootlaces and dropped them on the floor in front of his cell. I slammed the door on him and locked it, then gave Sam my full attention.

He was crouching against the doorway that led to the interior of the station. His hackles were up and the whine was tuning itself into a growl, his attack growl. I studied him for a moment, then unflipped my holster and took out my gun. I went to the door, braced myself for whatever might be waiting, then threw it open and jumped inside and low, crouching to one side down clear of the light.

Sam came past me, barking savagely. I waited for thirty seconds but no human voice was added to the noise. I knew the crisis was past. I stood up and flicked the light switch, flooding the room with greenish fluorescent light, and I realized why Sam had been alert.

The place had been torn apart.

Drawers were lying on the floor upside down, files were flopped about with their contents spilled out. The stationery cupboard had been rifled.

I looked up at the wall where our little safe stood. It was gone. Too tough to be opened in a hurry, it had been prised right out of the wall and removed.

I told Sam "easy" and he came to me. "Old buddy, they're still in town," I told him.

10

I did the obvious things first. I opened the counter flap and went through to check the space in front of the desk. There was nobody there. They had come in, and presumably left again, through one of the screen windows. It had been cut very neatly. I wondered whether it had been done by the same knife that had let the life out of Ross Winslow.

Once I checked inside, I threw the front door open and told Sam "seek." He ran his hunting circles around the place until I was sure there was nobody out there within a hundred yards of me. I walked out to the edge of the road and checked both ways. There was no car in sight and none could have hidden in the bush; it's too low all along there. I whistled Sam back and went back inside the station. It was depressing to stand there amid the clutter. This couldn't happen in a bigger department where there was at least one spare man to look after the station. I felt for a moment that I ought to strip the police flash off my shirtsleeves and sew on a Mickey Mouse.

But that phase passed. For one thing, the mosquitoes were pouring in through the open window where the screen had been cut. I closed the glass on them. It didn't help the temperature any—it was close to a hundred inside—but the mosquitoes can drive you right off your head after a while.

I checked around the room. Everything had been turned over, except for one or two items that were still intact. The gun rack had been left untouched, the shotgun and rifle still locked in place. The contents of the cupboard beneath it had been strewn around everywhere. So it had not been thieves. Thieves would have picked up the station hardware, the guns and the typewriters. No, these people had been looking for something else. And it figured to be the envelope that Angela Masters had given me. I picked up the telephone to call Murphy's house. Somebody was talking on the line, some semidrunk telling Bertha about a blue boat with a red sail that he had seen that day. I cut in over him and he said "Whooozis?" a couple of times. I told him, "Police chief, clear the line, please." He swore and hung up.

Bertha said, "Hi, Reid, up the station, are you?"

"Yeah, I just got in. Tell me, please, is Murph there?"

"No. He's gone out. I told him to go up the Legion and get himself a glass of beer. He's that upset, he don't know what to do with himself."

"Good idea." I didn't mean it. I needed all the help I could get. Murphy drunk was no help at all. "How long's he been gone?" I tried.

"About an hour." She broke off, searching for the proper words. "I figure you better call him soon if you want a sensible answer."

"Good thinking. They're likely having a remembrance for Ross Winslow."

"That's what Murph said," she confirmed.

I thanked her and asked her to leave me a line clear for a while. "In fact, the hell with it, I'm going to be here most of the time. Unplug the phone down there and get some sleep. I'll mind the store."

114

She sounded tired as she answered and I remembered she was close to Murphy's age, damn near old enough to be my mother. "I b'lieve I will," she said.

We exchanged very civilized good nights. I depressed the phone button, then let go and phoned the Legion Hall. There was a lot of noise at the other end. It sounded like a hundred drinking parties I'd been on in the service. Men fulfilling their god-given duty of making themselves goddamn stupid with booze. I asked for Murphy. There was a delay and then he was there, sounding angry. "What's up now?"

"We had visitors at the station. Guys with pinch bars, took the place to pieces."

His voice rose excitedly. "Did they get it?"

I told him, "No. But it's gonna take a month to put things back together again."

Murphy swore. It was soft but definite. "What in hell is things coming to, Reid? First the goddamn boat gets took off you. Then Ross gets killed in it. Now the station's tore all up. Where in hell is it gonna end?"

A mosquito had realized that lunch was on and settled lovingly on my cheek to dig in. I slapped it. Murphy heard the noise.

"Now what?" he almost snarled it.

I kept my temper. It was a hot night, even if you weren't almost sixty and crippled up and bereaved and confronted with a piece of malice that would rob you of your Sunday off. "Just a bug. The shopbreakers came in through the front screen." On impulse I added, "But they're wasting their time. I'm gonna mail that envelope to the attorney general's office, care of myself. Then on Monday I'll drive down there and pick it up and take it down to Straiton Chemicals."

"Are you out of your mind?" Murphy's voice was a hiss of horror. "What did the goddamn M'rines teach you about security? You're not dealing with dummies, you know, you're

115

dealing with the big time; these guys may have the station bugged."

I slapped another mosquito. "I'm certain they do, the kind that bite," I said.

"You're crazy," he said.

"Take it easy. This isn't the Russian embassy," I told him.

Murphy made no attempt to hide his anger. "I'm not wasting time arguing with you. I'm not coming in tonight, no matter what. I'm gonna have a few beers. *Quite* a few beers, in fact. I'll be in tomorrow, not too early. I'll tidy up then."

I said, "Thanks, Murph. Enjoy," and hung up.

I stood looking at the phone for a long moment, then I realized what I had to do. I weighed the meaning of every word we had exchanged and finally I went over to the gun rack, unlocked the guns, and did what had to be done. After that, I prepared my bait. I picked up a few sheets of paper at random from the mess on the floor, folded them in half, and put them in a manila envelope a size larger than the one Angela Masters had given me. I wrote "Chief Bennett, Murphy's Harbour Police Department, C/O Attorney General's Department" and put the Toronto address down. I sealed it and stamped it and slipped the whole thing back into the front of my shirt.

I whistled Sam to heel and went out the back way, checking on Eddy, who was snoring harmoniously. It was the third time he'd been inside for drunkenness since I'd been chief. This time he'd probably get thirty days to complete his snoring.

I put Sam in the car and drove down to the post office on the main drag. For a moment I considered putting the flasher on, but that would have been too corny. I figured my actions would be obvious enough.

It was close to ten at night. The street was quiet. A young couple was walking arm in arm down by the waterside, looking at the ripples of sunfish coming up to feed on the bugs that

116

fell in the water under the lights. I glanced up and down, let Sam out of the car, in case I should be lucky enough to have someone try to grab the letter off me as I mailed it, and stepped out in front of the mail box.

The phony letter went through the slot with a faint whoosh. And then I heard the sound I'd been half expecting. From a dark space between two houses a woman's voice said, "Officer!"

I turned toward the sound. "Hello, Miss Masters, I've been looking for you," I said. I was so delighted I felt like hugging the bitch. Here we had come full circle. It had all started out with her knowing nothing and needing help from me. Now it had switched. As sure as God made the Province of Ontario she had all the answers I needed. And now she had come back, trying to undo the one slip she had made, handing me that envelope. Without that, she and Pardoe and whoever did the throat cutting in their organization would have been on their way.

Before she could answer I bored in. "Where's Pardoe?"

She lied, of course, but at such a rate that I could tell she was under pressure. "I don't know. But it doesn't matter. I'm going home. I want my envelope back."

"Forget it," I told her. "You're staying with me until I get Pardoe and find who slit a man's throat this afternoon." She said, "I don't know what you mean," and meant it.

"Then I'm arresting you on suspicion of complicity in the murder." I reached out and took hold of her wrist. I expected her to pull away or argue but she didn't even struggle. I wondered even then if she was acting under instructions. I was holding her left wrist and she had nothing in her right hand, no weapon, and she didn't look as if she knew any martial arts, but I took no chances. I glanced around again. I had canceled any chance of an ambush by staying close to the wall of the house, alongside her. The only place anyone could be

117

hiding was down the side of the house where I'd sent Sam to check. The only place to take a shot at me was from out on the lake. Even a sniper sight couldn't have picked me off from out there.

The streetlight had given her extra shadows, but those under her eyes were the deepest, the most real.

"Let's go," I said.

She laughed, a real, open feminine laugh.

I felt my control beginning to slip. She was too calm. It felt like once we were talking to a couple of prisoners in a village in Viet Nam. They had been calm, right up until the counterattack started. I should have learned from that, never to trust anyone too much at ease in a difficult spot. But she was a woman and looking almost beautiful. She had fixed her makeup. Her hair was a blond fountain and her high cheekbones gave her class to burn. On any night, any other night, I would have been turned on. Tonight I was just worried.

I whistled Sam and put her in the back seat with him beside her. If she resented it, she didn't let it show. She sat back as if I were a taxi driver taking her to a ball and said nothing until I reached the station.

I left the lights out inside the car and turned Sam out to search. He ran back and forth around the station until I knew it was clear. Then I got out and unlocked the back door. She didn't come out and I had to reach in and grab her wrist. Now she came, slithering up out of the seat and draping herself all over me. Her knee slid between mine but I sidestepped quickly. "Cut it out," I said curtly.

Her voice was languorous, like an expensive hooker I ended up with on my first night of R and R in Hong Kong. "You're a very attractive man," she said.

Her free hand had crept around my waist, as if she were trying to embrace me, but I guessed she was feeling for the pocket where I carried my stick, hoping the envelope would be

118

there. I said, "Suppose I go along with this malarkey and then still arrest you and don't give you the envelope. Will you still feel this amorous?" That touched the nerve. She tensed her arm and swung at me. "You dirty sonofabitch."

I trapped her other arm. Sam saw the motion and growled at her but did nothing, as I gave him no command. "Cut the sweet talk, you're making my dog upset," I told her. "Let's go inside." She was sobbing now, out of pure frustration. "What does it take to get my envelope back? What?"

She brought her knee up but I was sideways on and she just bumped my thigh. I told her, "Cool it or I'll get Sam to bite you where you don't want biting."

I let go of her hands and she lowered them to her sides and stared at me, looking like a petulant three year old. "What's wrong with you? Are you gay? I'm a good-looking woman. I know I am. Men have told me I am."

"You're great. I'm straight. And this is a work night," I said. The jangle of the words pleased me. I thought I was getting through to her at last. I could see the rest of the pieces of my puzzle snapping together as neatly as my cuffs would snap on the wrist of the man who had killed Winslow. What a dreamer.

She snuffled again and I asked her, "Where's Pardoe?" She didn't look up. I led her by the elbow through the door, with Sam behind us, then closed the door and sat her down on the kitchen chair next to the empty cell. What a fool. I should have put her inside it and locked the door. But I was still trying to do what I had been told to do, treat her like a citizen, a human being with equal rights, not an enemy.

She said at last, "They've got him."

"Who's they?"

"Two men. They came to the motel just after you took me back there." She wasn't acting now. I'd seen her act, and this wasn't it.

119

"Did they come into your unit?"

She nodded. "They came in and told me to do what they said or they would mark my face up."

"What did you do?"

She looked at me, flat and level, her voice tense. "I did what they told me. They looked as if they meant what they said."

"So what happened?"

"They sat and smoked and we waited, and after a while Derek came back, alone."

"Derek Pardoe?"

I broke the thread of her story to check whether she could pick it up again. "Where had he been all night?" I could guess the answer. First, when he jumped out of the boat, he had been lost. He didn't know the lake and he wouldn't be sure of his directions back to the highway. On top of which, he was scared. Somebody knew enough about him to have a boat set up to intercept him at Murphy's Harbour. That meant he didn't know who he could trust. He would have stayed away from any lighted cottages, probably waiting until daylight to make his way back toward the highway after he had oriented himself again from what he could remember seeing in the twilight the night before. But the girl didn't have an answer for me anyway.

"I didn't get a chance to ask him." It could have been a story, but she was too angry.

"Why not?"

"When he saw them he tried to fight, and they hit him. They hit him hard."

"How hard? Did he bleed?"

"Worse than that." She pantomimed it for me and even at second hand it brought back enough real-life memories to chill me.

"His eyes rolled up; they were just whites. It was awful."

"Was he breathing?"

"Yes." She nodded frantically. "Yes, but it wasn't normal, it was kind of a snuffling sound."

"So tell me where he is and I'll go get him."

She grabbed my sleeve, for real this time, no hint of seduction in the motion. "They told me they would kill me if I came back with you. They just want the envelope."

I pointed at Sam, who was sitting watching us, his tongue hanging out. "I've got Sam, I've got guns, I can take care of them."

"No." She moaned the word, shaking her head. Then she looked up at me and whispered, "Please. Please, for Derek's sake."

"So tell me what they look like."

She gave me a description that would have fit only about half the visitors to Murphy's Harbour, the male half. One was tall, one wasn't. They had light summer clothes, city clothes, not casual, and two-tone shoes. That made them American.

"They're not at the motel; I was up there. Where are they?"

"They're in a cottage. They took me there, blindfolded."

It was my turn to laugh. "You watch too much television, what are you talking about, blindfolded?"

Her face stiffened with anger. "They took a towel out of the bathroom and when we got in the car they covered my eyes."

"Whose car?"

"My car, of course." She had no hesitation, it was true. But it left unanswered the question of how two mob heavies had found their way to the motel, how they had got there, what they had done with the car they arrived in. Could it be there were three of them? Two operatives and a third man to drive their car?

"Did they put Pardoe in with you?"

"Yes. He was lying across the seat. He was unconscious, burbling as he breathed. I kept asking if he was all right."

"And what did they say?"

She winced and covered her breast with a little reflexive motion.

"One of them elbowed me in the breast. It hurt."

"Nice guys." I tried to sound angry. "How long were you in the car with them?"

She shrugged. "It felt like hours."

"It couldn't have been, you're back here already," I reminded her.

"I don't know how long," she said. "Why is it important?"

"It might give me a fix on the radius I have to search."

She tried but gave up with another shrug. "I don't know, maybe ten minutes."

"Was there a radio in the car?"

Her eyes narrowed in puzzlement. "Why?"

"Did it play through two tunes, ten tunes, one commercial, what?"

She clenched her fists and gave a short, angry shake to her hands. "Really, what do you think I am? Derek was hurt, I was frightened. I wasn't listening to the radio."

"Okay, tell me about the cottage, or did they keep the towel on your face then as well?"

She thought about that one for a moment, then said, "It was neat. The room I was put in had broadloom on the floor."

"What could you see out of the window?"

"The blinds were drawn. I think there were shutters outside the window as well. No light was coming in, anyway."

"And they had the lights on?"

She nodded.

"Electric?"

"Of course." She was a New Yorker—what other kind of light was there? She didn't know that half our cottage country still made do with propane or even kerosene lights. So she'd been in a modern place, not too remote.

"What could you hear outside?"

"You mean what kind of noises?" She was puzzled again, off balance at being asked questions when she had been told to get her envelope and come back.

"Was there any sound of traffic, or a train, or running water, what?"

"I could hear a cow mooing." She was getting desperate again. "Listen, you can't keep me here. I have to get back."

"Back where?"

"I don't know." She almost shrieked it. "I don't know. I'm to be picked up."

"Fine. I'll come with you." At last I could see a break coming my way. "Where are they picking you up. I'll take over and we'll get this thing sorted out."

"It won't work." She was close to tears. "These are rough people. All they want is that envelope. Then they said they'll let me get help for Derek. They just want that envelope."

"It's not that easy. They've killed a man. They won't mind killing you and Pardoe, both. You've got to take me where I can get at them. Where are you meeting them, here?"

She ignored me. "Just give me the envelope. Please."

"I can't. They know I can't. If they've given you a deadline I'm just going to have to put you in a cell and see what they do."

Her head dipped, tearfully. I've seen too many tears from too many crime victims to feel sympathy. Sure she was in a mess. But so was Winslow. So was Pardoe. I had to keep her where she was, as bait. I played it the way I've played it ever since those bikies played rough. No violence. Nothing but cool, calm police work. I stood and watched, vigilant but not hostile as her hand dipped into the purse she was carrying, groping for a tissue. I knew that if she came out with a gun, Sam would have it out of her hand as fast as I could tell him "Fight!"

But she didn't bring out a gun. It was a canister, small, dull,

123

and businesslike. As she pointed it I tried to grab for it, tried to speak to Sam, but nothing came out of me. A cloud of peppery stinging, stupefying Mace dissolved the edges of reality. Her voice kept coming, low and apologetic. The words didn't reach me then, but later, when I was over it all, I remembered them. She was saying she was sorry.

The jet turned away momentarily and I heard a low anxious whining out of Sam. I tried to ask her to leave him alone, but she couldn't have heard me. My words were drying up and dying away like an old phonograph running down in mid-record. Then the floor of the corridor came up and took hold of me.

I was aware that she was leaning down over me. Her form was there, vague as a figure seen through frosted glass. She was still talking, but it meant nothing at all. My brains, my coordination were all gone. I felt her unfastening my handcuffs pouch, and then nothing at all.

11

I swam upward through a pool of something as dark as ink and twice as bitter into the worst hangover I had ever known. I was lying face down on cool concrete. My left hand was underneath me but my right was extended up and back off the edge of the explored world.

I lay there for a while, treasuring the coolness of the concrete against my face, then my brain stopped slopping around in my head and I rolled slowly up on to my left hand and took stock.

The first thing I realized was that I was handcuffed to a cell bar by my right wrist. The second thing was that Sam was in worse shape than I was. He lay about six feet away, his muzzle in a pool of saliva. The sight made my stomach roll. He was alive, retching mechanically as if it were another of the tricks I had taught him.

With my left hand I patted my pockets for keys. They were gone. My wallet was still there, and my gun and nightstick. Weak as I was, I breathed a little sigh of relief about that. Whether the girl had been dumb or humane, she had given me a chance to protect myself. Her buddies from the cottage with carpet on the floor would not be able to come back and use me as a football. Probably they would slap her around a little for being so forgetful, but at least I was going to be able to find her and help her, once I got out of the mess I was in.

With my faculties regrouping I put together the bits of information I'd gotten from her, either in her words or her actions. For one thing, that can of Mace had come from the station. I hadn't stopped to check everything, but the ammunition cupboard was torn open and it must have been taken out. That meant she was in touch with the guys who had ripped the place off. At worst, it meant she was part of their set-up. Then I dismissed that thought as I patted the holster. She would never have left me the gun if she had been working with them.

I wiped my mouth on my sleeve and sat up. This loosened a great jagged chunk of pain in my head and it flopped around inside like a rusty shovel in a coal bucket. I winced and vomited again, managing to avoid getting any on me.

I sat still for a while, working out what to do. There wasn't much. It was no good trying to shoot the cuffs off; they're carbon steel. A lead bullet would ricochet off without denting them, but it might easily come tumbling back through my damn fool head. For security's sake I took out my gun, unflipped it to make sure it was loaded, and set it down next to my left hand. I'm a good shot with either hand. If it came to a showdown, I'd make them sorry they'd tried.

I listened to the quiet. I could hear bullfrogs larrupping away, and a whippoorwill flogging away at his old complaint, but not a car, not a human voice. I cursed the councilor who had sold the township this piece of wasteland for a police office site. We should be on Main Street, where we could be useful to tourists and vice bloody versa. I had an idea. At least it seemed like an idea at first. I took out my whistle and blew it in three blasts, over and over. All it did was make Sam roll hurt eyes in a mute plea for me to stop. That, and wake Eddy

Crowfoot from his well-earned drunken sleep to swear at me in a flood of mixed French, English, and Ojibway. He stood up and pounded on his bars like your friendly neighborhood bear. By now the booze was wearing off and he could see what was going down. He immediately claimed the glory.

"Hey. I beat you, huh?" He reeled with laughter, holding onto the bars to keep upright, pointing at Sam as if he was the funniest sight in the world. "Him too, eh? eh?" He stopped to vomit. "Goddamn whiskey," he said cheerfully, as if talking about the weather, then went back to his laughing and cheering, ending up by favoring us with a full-blooded war whoop that made up for the pain I'd caused him by whistling. He stopped and pointed his index finger at Sam, cocking his thumb like a little boy playing guns. "Bang," he said jovially. "He's rabid, Reid, lookit that, he's foamin'. You should shoot 'im."

There was nothing for me to do but sit quiet and wait for him to go to sleep again, then wait for a hungover Murphy to come in tomorrow morning and let me out of my problem. For the moment I was only worried about Sam. He was in danger of dehydrating. I tried to think of some way of helping Sam get to his feet and come in to the cell and lap himself some water from the toilet. Eddy didn't help. He kept up his chant like the drunk at the lodge meeting who wears the lampshade and his wife's coat. "Hey, lookit that dog. Worse'n me. Why you don't lock 'im up, Chief? Hey, Chief, lock 'im up."

I managed to coax Sam to move over to me. His legs were rubbery and he almost fell over a couple of times in the ten feet. And once he reached me, he didn't know what to do. There is no snappy command you can give any dog to find himself some water and drink. No matter how well trained, he's like a baby when you get him off the information he knows how to handle. He looked at me in a puzzled way and heaved some more. I pushed him toward the cell door but he didn't get the message, just lay down again and went on retching.

Eddy was howling with laughter, having the time of his easy-to-please life. It went on until I had stood all I could. I was almost ready to threaten him with my pistol. And that's where everything snapped into focus for me. It was time to be a soldier again. Police tactics had gotten me nowhere. I was outgunned, outmaneuvered, outnumbered, and so far, out-thought. It was time to throw the book away and use all the weapons I had instead of giving the other people all the breaks the law said they should have.

I started by turning to Eddy and staring down his eyes until he wound down the volume, dropped his eyes, and went back to his bunk, and eventually to sleep.

Almost two hours passed. Once I thought I heard move-ment in the front of the police station and I was torn between the urge to shout and call for help and the fear that it might be somebody going over the ruins one more time, looking for the envelope. If it was the heavies back again, I'd just as soon not draw attention to myself. So I sat very still and waited and after a while became certain that I was mistaken, nobody had been there.

Sometime after midnight I heard a car pull in beside the station. I took up my gun and waited. It was the same old heart-hammering wait I'd been through before. You can work out the whole scenario before it happens. You see the door fly open and the bullets coming at you like hailstones. You duck and twist but they reach out and catch you, curving like baseballs to find you and deliver their message. No matter how many villages you search, how many times you are point man in the tall grass, how many times you search a building that has been broken into, you can always anticipate the action. I turned sideways to the door, making myself as narrow a target as possible, and waited.

The door creaked open, an inch at a time, while my life shortened. And then the scared, honest face of young George appeared. "Christ, Reid. What happened?"

"Chemical warfare. I'll tell you later," I told him. "First thing, take a look under the gun rack on the floor in the other office. There's a spare set of keys, including cuff keys."

He shook his head and vanished through the door into the office. I heard him swear once, then nothing, except for his feet crunching over the papers and mess. He was back in a minute with the spare key chain.

I took it off him and shook it around until I got the tiny cuff key, then I unlocked my right wrist and stood and rubbed it for a moment. The cuff had been tight enough to cramp into the bone and now that I no longer had to live with it, I allowed myself the luxury of remembering how much it had hurt.

I unsnapped the cuff from the cell bar and put the handcuffs back in my pouch. Then I stuffed the keys in my pocket, holstered my gun, and said "thanks" again.

"Welcome," George said. He was checking everything with his eyes. He looked like a Sioux in one of those old Remington paintings. I wondered if his eyes could see something a white policeman would miss. He said, "Can you tell me what's going on?"

"Some guys worked the station over, looking for evidence in the case."

"Well, they're too late. I took it all to T'rannah."

I didn't spoil his illusions. The more people thought the envelope was in the city, the safer we would all be. I stooped down and took Sam's collar. "C'mon boy . . ." He came with me to the seatless toilet in the second cell. It was spotlessly clean. I do a Marine Corps job of housecleaning. I flushed it for him and dipped my hand into the water so he'd get the idea. Gently, groggily, he began to lap. I told him "easy boy"

129

and left him lapping. He seemed able to understand me, coming back to life inch by inch, the way Eddy Crowfoot would the next morning. His respiration seemed normal. I figured he would be all right in time.

Only we didn't have much time.

George asked, "What are you gonna do?"

I looked at him, young, fit, even eager. "It depends a bit on you," I told him. "Could you stick around for a while and help?"

"Of course," he shrugged his slim shoulders. He had already driven four hundred miles at illegal speeds to do me a favor. He had to be back at work the next morning at eight, but he was on my side all the way. At some point I would have to make sure the township recognized what he had done.

For now I said, "Great. Lemme tell you what needs doing." I filled him in very briefly on what had happened, while I dug through the ruins in the office for the ledger I needed. I found it. "In here you'll find the home address and phone number of everyone with a cottage in our district." He looked at me without speaking, every inch the Hollywood Indian. "And we know that Pardoe came up here to visit someone."

"So?" He was mystified.

"So let's see if we've got any cottages belonging to people who live in New York, that's the city."

"Just New York?" A tracker's question—just marten? not fisher or beaver or lynx?

"For openers, but make a list of any Americans, we'll call them all if we don't hit the right guy from New York."

"Seems like a long chance," he said, but he was already looking about him for a paper and pencil.

"It *is* a long chance. But that's the only kind you get in this business."

I went to the large-scale map we kept on the wall. It had been ripped off at the top and was hanging down from one pin at the bottom. I took it over to the counter top and spread it out. My head was still hurting, but I found that I could clear it by concentrating hard. I studied the map until everything else was gone. Using my thumb and forefinger as a pair of dividers I drew a circle on the map that took in all the territory within a twenty minute's drive of the Canadiana Motel excluding places that lay up or down the highway. She would have traffic sounds if she had driven there. It added up to something more than a semicircle with a five-mile radius. Then I eliminated all of the areas close to major roads or waterfalls or anything else that would have made a noise Angela Masters would have remembered. I cut out anywhere close to a lake big enough to have powerboats. And finally I cut out any place that did not have open fields close by.

It left a hell of a lot of territory open to me. Next I drew the same kind of circle with Main Street as its center. It cut down the possible area by a lot more.

I stood looking at the space in front of me on the map and did another mental debriefing on what she had said to me while she was here. I remembered carpet. She had mentioned carpet on the floor of the place she was kept.

I picked up the phone book off the floor and got the home number of the town building inspector. It took ten rings to wake him up. He sounded out of it. I told him, "Chief Bennett, Murphy's Harbour police. I'm sorry to bother you at this time of night but we have an emergency."

"Emergency?" His voice juggled the word like an unexploded grenade.

"Yes. I need some help in finding the person who murdered Ross Winslow." It always pays to play a high card early. This time I got the distinct impression I was talking to my own armpit.

"Ross Winslow?"

"Yes. I need some information from the town files and you're the man who has it. Can you open up the office for me?"

"Tonight?" His voice ran up and off the top of the scale. "Right away if possible."

There was a blustering noise, muffled by bedclothes as he explained to his wife what kind of chowderhead I was. Then he came back on. "It's not possible. This is the middle of the night, Saturday night. The office doesn't open till Monday."

I had stood still long enough. I needed help, the whole of Murphy's Harbour needed help. I was going to get it. "Before you get too cute, let me tell you that if I have to wait until Monday I will call your wife on Monday morning and tell her where you and your secretary park your car during the lunch hour. Okay?" I thundered out the "okay" like a gunshot, both barrels. I let him sit there with the sound ringing through his startled head for a couple of seconds, then I dropped to a conversational tone and said, "Ring me from the office, in no more than ten minutes. Got that?"

Another pause, a defeated sigh, a face-saving line. "If there's anything I can do to help catch them bastards, I'll do it. I'll call from the office." I hung up and checked on George.

He had four numbers for me. All were from New York State. Only one was from the city. I added more requests. "Better put the location and lot number against the phone numbers, they might fit with the other thing I'm looking for. Meanwhile, I'll call this guy." I rang the number and waited while the phone did its long-distance sighing and clicking, then rang.

A man picked it up, an angry man. "Who's this?" he wanted to know.

I told him and listened while little squawks of disapproval came burrowing down the phone line to my ear. "I've got a murder investigation going on and I need to know if you have been up at your cottage this weekend."

"Murder?" That put him in a different gear. "No, we haven't, off'cer."

"And is anyone else using your place in your absence?"

Nobody was. If any sonofabitch was hanging around there I had his permission to kick his ass.

I thanked him, hung up, and drew a line through his name. The next number was the same. I was about to try the third when the phone rang. It was the building inspector.

"What did you want to know?" he asked, very civilly.

"Thank you, Lloyd. I have reason to believe that a man I want to talk to is staying at a summer place in our area. I'm not sure where, but I have some indications. Maybe you could help."

He said, "I'll try," but left it an unfinished sentence, and then tailed it off in a rush. "Listen, you won't phone my wife, eh, there's nothin' in it with my secretary. She just likes to get out of the office, ya know."

"Forget about it. All I need is some help," I told him. It wasn't a time for compassion, just high-handedness. This time, I was out to win.

"Thanks, Chief." It was like dealing with a child.

"You're welcome. Now . . . what I have is a list of locations that this place might be. Have you got a map there?" There was a pause while he found one, then I gave him some more details. "I've narrowed it down to about five sections of highway. Got a pencil?"

He needed one, which took more time. I looked up and found George studying me as if I had just discovered radium. I winked at him and he dived right back into the ledger. Lloyd found his pencil and I read off the names of the highways and the approximate sections. "What I'm looking for is a bigger place, set back away from the main road, somewhere quiet."

"Gotcha." He was so anxious to please I could hardly finish my instructions.

I choked him off. "And what's going to make it particularly great is if this place has a farm next to it, or is on a farm, for that matter."

His anxiety to please was fighting a losing battle with re-

133

ality. His voice was quietly despondent. "Hell, that's not a lot to go on."

"I've got more, but it's not much."

"Yeah?" He sounded like a swimmer who has just made the length of the pool—underwater.

"Yeah. This place has carpet on the floor, broadloom. That should make it a fancier grade of place than most we have around here."

"I've got carpet wall-to-wall in my summer place," he told me. The line breathed in and out while I considered telling him that not too many of the public had the ability to pass out building permits, and so many builders anxious to please them. He caught the silence out of the air like a football. "Of course, my place *is* kinda fancy."

"It's beautiful," I told him, in a tone pitched exactly right for the second level of message, the collection of the debt he owed Murphy's Harbour. It paid off.

"I know what you mean." He almost crowed. I could imagine his scrawny little neck stretched up as he shouted. He went into the second verse. "Just you hold the phone . . ."

I headed him off. "Can't do that, I need it. You call me back when you find something, okay?"

"Oh Kay . . ." he made two words out of it and clattered the phone down with the first real excitement he had shown in life since he realized his secretary's husband was not living up to his contract. I grinned and hung up the phone and then George's voice was rising with excitement.

"Hey. Reid, I found it!" He picked up the ledger bodily and carried it to the counter in front of me.

I read the words under his forefinger and gave a rebel yell. "You're right, goddamn it! Why didn't I think of it?"

He was laughing like a jackpot winner. "It figures. It figures, Reid. The place had to be on an island or they wouldn't have needed to hire a boat to take them there."

134

We pounded one another on the arm a couple of times, blindly, while I read the whole of the story. "Henry J. Clemence, Residence, White Plains, New York. Business Address, Straiton Chemicals, Madison Avenue."

George was still chortling. "How about that luck, eh? The business address right there. I can't believe it. Why'd he do that?"

I shrugged. "It's about time something good happened to us guys, and I guess he was thinking his family might be up here and him at work. If anything went wrong, that's where we'd have to reach him."

I had stopped laughing. Playtime was ended. I was orchestrating the best way to handle the call. A man rich enough to own a property six hundred miles from where he lived was not very likely to want to hold long midnight conversations with coppers. I would have to be careful.

"Don't count on him telling me why Pardoe was up here," I warned.

"Why not?" George still believed in happy endings, in right guys winning and other TV kinds of sentimentality.

"He doesn't have to tell me a thing." I stood for a moment, rubbing my eyes, and as I did so, I realized that they had stopped burning. I was over the worst of the Mace.

George brought me back to this time and place. "He doesn't have a phone on his island."

I opened my eyes and thought about it for a while that way. "I'll check he's not home in New York, then take a turn up there." Cool. Definitely cool for a guy who has just realized that about half the pieces of his puzzle are snapping together like magic. I picked up the phone and called White Plains. It rang seventeen times before I hung up. He couldn't answer. He was too far away, up here in Ontario, waiting for Pardoe to come boating up to his dock with a piece of plastic that answered all his problems. Or set him a whole bunch of new ones. I set the phone down with relief. There was something real to do. "Listen, George. I'm going to get this guy up and talk to him. Can you carry on here?"

He was dejected. "I'd rather come with you."

He was ready to swim lakes, trek through swamps, leap tall buildings at a single bound. And I was a louse. But I was doing the right thing. I needed him here in case this hot lead cooled right out when we rode three miles up the waterway and found the Clemence family had gone back to White Plains, leaving us with nothing. Someone had to stay and play office, and someone had to risk his neck. And I was the only one getting compensated for risking his neck, however unlikely that seemed. "Better you should stay here. Lloyd will be, calling in with some information, and there's the whole book to go through for more guys from Straiton when we find this is the wrong one."

"What if it's the right one? What if you need help right there?" He stood, bouncing on the balls of his feet with excitement he couldn't keep down.

"It won't be." I threw some cold water. "This time tomorrow, when you can't keep your eyes open and we know that it's not any of half a dozen guys like this one but we have to keep looking, you'll be glad you kept on while I was off screwing around."

"Like hell," he said, but he was coming around.

"It's more important to be here, please."

"Okay. What needs doing, besides answering the phone and more reading?" He wasn't happy, but he was settling.

"Call Fullwell and tell him that Angela Masters was here, Maced me and Sam, and that I would like him to come back and join us, as soon as he can."

He took down the phone number, still disgusted, writing in a sloping left-handed scrawl. "That's not much police work, one phone call and a bunch of reading."

136

"Believe me . . ." I started, but he waved me away.

"Okay, I'll do it."

I picked up my notes and went to the back door. "Back soon."

"Yeah," he said.

I went into the corridor and found my hat lying on the floor where it had rolled when I was Maced. My head was hurting, but clear. Sam was following me, weak himself, but still anxious to see what was going to happen. I felt better just watching him, until he fell over as his front legs gave out.

That decided me. I would take him home first. I had not even thought about the card hidden in his pen. That would come when we got there. He could do the guard job he was trained for. I would give him some milk in that important dish of his, wash the last of the chemical out of his system.

I whistled him and he came to heel, like a drunken soldier falling in on parade, hoping to get by from memory rather than acuteness. I got to the door and paused. I was no longer sure what was outside, what was waiting for me. I only knew that I was through playing by the rules. From the moment I was blitzed with my own Mace, I was ready to play their way. It meant I had to sit Sam down and switch off the lights. First the inside, then the outside lights. Then I inched the door open. There was no light showing. Unless the other side was using an infra-red sniper's sight, I was okay. But I had been shot at before by guys with sniper sights. So I didn't take any chances. I flung the door open and rolled out, whistling Sam after me. Nothing happened. That still left me the problem of getting into the patrol car. It could have been covered the same way, but I was beginning to doubt it.

Sam landed on collapsible legs and rolled away from me. When he stood up I gave him the command to search and he left me, beating away with all his might, up and down, all around the station. He was slow but I trusted him.

I called him back and got into the patrol car, with him on the passenger seat. He flopped there and I drove off, spurting gravel in a way that must have made George look up from his book-searching in wonderment.

I drove back through town, slowing down opposite the mailbox. It was as I expected. Someone had pried it out of the wall and it lay surrounded by a clutter of postcards and mail. Without stopping, I knew my envelope would be gone. "Murphy was on the ball," I told Sam as we drove. "They've got a line right into the station." Sam only looked up, then slept again like a drunk taking the cure. I was angry about the mailbox. It had been my trap. I had planted that letter and had planned to stake it out and catch the man who came to rip it off. And then that damn woman with her angelic face and diabolical manners had made a monkey out of me.

I contemplated their next move. Obviously, they would search the house. And they wouldn't find the envelope, so they would stake it out for me. The thought cheered me in a negative kind of way. At least I knew where the trap was set, even if I was the bait instead of the trip spring.

I thought it through as I drove. They wouldn't shoot me down. They wanted that envelope of Angela Masters's. I had a fighting chance. And I was ready to fight.

I parked the car in front of the house, gunning the motor before it died. Might as well act stupid. On my record, they would be expecting it.

I got out and called Sam after me. He came along, listlessly but gaining strength. The car ride had shaken him and he stopped to throw up once before climbing the steps.

I tried the front door. It was unlocked, the way I had left it. I made a show of fumbling with the door and acting noisy. And at the same time I unflipped my holster and took out my .38.

Then I threw the door open and stepped in and down, out of the light from the doorway. My hand thrust Sam forward

138

with the little twist I gave him to signify "search." At the same time I told him "speak!"

Even sick, Sam was magnificent. His snarls and barks filled the house like gunfire. On his unsteady feet he moved from room to room with a stiff-legged ferocity that made his long claws clash on the old pine plank flooring.

Within seconds I knew what was happening.

I heard a yell. It wasn't as dignified as a shout or as horrifying as a scream. It was a yell of alarm, from the dark by the back door.

I charged in, shouting to Sam "fight!"

I waited ten seconds while the room was filled with the crash of falling furniture and the angry shouting of a frightened man.

Then I snapped on the light.

The intruder was big. He had a pallid moon face and dark hair. Sam was hanging on to his gun hand. But he was drowning in his own saliva and as I watched he lost his grip and fell away, shaking his great head angrily.

I shouted, "Hold it," but the man was wrapped up with Sam. He fired wildly, missing him by a foot, then turned and slammed one my way. I snap fired, aiming for the stopping portion of the target, the section of the torso that is painted solid black on the police revolver target.

He flew backward and his gun crashed back against the wall, then down to the floor.

I advanced on him, still wary, gun at the ready to hit him again, hard.

Sam was recovering. He moved in with me. His eyes were fixed on the man's face. His dead face. I reached the corpse and knelt beside him, feeling for the pulse in the throat. It was out of business.

I told Sam "seek" and he went off to check the rest of the house while I checked the body.

My bullet had entered the chest at the top inside corner of

139

his breast pocket. The entrance wound was a dull hole, one inch away from the breastbone, a hand's breadth below the inside of his collar bone. It had gone through his heart. I felt my neck prickle with an inhuman pride in what I had done. One shot! My Marine Corps instructor would have been proud of me.

Then I swore. The bullet had wiped away my advantage. I had no prisoner to question.

I stood up tall and waited for Sam to finish searching the house. There was no one there but me, Sam, and our dead man. I came away from the body and went to the fridge, reaching in for the milk. I poured some for Sam in a saucepan, the only utensil handy. The rest of the carton I drank.

12

I should not have searched the body. Normal, step-at-a-time police procedure dictated that I call another policeman, some independent party, and let him proceed with the homicide investigation. Then, after the photographs and the statements were taken and the body was moved away, I could have gone on with my investigation.

I knew the drill but I ignored it. I judged, from the speed with which things were happening, that something big was going to break soon. I wanted to be in on it. I had scores to repay. Not professional, but more effective than the long gray columns of rules set out in all the law books.

I rolled the body over, onto its bloody front, frowning at the width of the exit wound. That .38 of mine did ugly work. I wasn't sorry for the hood. His gun would have made a bigger hole in me. I eased his billfold out of his hip pocket, trying to avoid the blood that soaked the whole of his back. Inside I found three hundred and fifty eight dollars in American money. There was a New York State driver's license in the name of Frederick Morse. There were a couple of photographs of the dead man, taken a year of two before when he was thinner. There was a matchbook from a New York City restaurant with a phone number scrawled on it and the name "Gina."

I made a note of the man's name and address and of the phone number. Then I tore the corner of a page out of my notebook and wrote "Searched, R. Bennett" and thrust it inside the wallet. Then I stuffed it back in the hip pocket, having to dig it down deep past the puffiness of the dead, collapsed buttocks.

I checked the man's pants pockets, but they were empty. Not a key, not a Kleenex. And what was more, there was no holster for the heavy automatic he had fired at me. That meant he had carried it in his hands, maybe wrapped up inside the light windbreaker that was hanging over the back of the chair beside him. It meant he had not walked far. Which meant his friends might be close at hand. Which meant fear for me.

I rolled him back the way he had been and looked at the wound. It was a pity I wasn't Matt Dillon, that my bullet had not clipped his hand neatly, leaving him alive and well and talkative, anxious to help. Instead, that neat black full stop in the corner of his breast pocket had ended him, forever.

I reached down and brushed the wound with a fingertip. And as I did so, I heard and felt a paper crinkle. I reached into the bloody pocket and pulled out the first real clue of the entire case.

It was a folded slip of paper. I opened it and read "*Mary Sue*. Admitted 4:35 P.M. North Lock" in Murphy's spidery writing. Below it was the stamp of the police office property receipt.

I gripped the paper, waving it in front of the dead man's face in a gesture of triumph. Even dead, he had given me the news I wanted.

And it all figured. The *Mary Sue*. That was the boat that had given Crazy Eddy the money to buy his mickey and his draft beers. No doubt they hadn't planned it that way, but their money had created the diversion that took me away from the station while the crew took their time cleaning the place out. That piece of paper would have been the perfect alibi except for the sharp eyes of young George, who had seen them in our section earlier in the day.

I slipped the piece of paper between the pages of my notebook, then went to the light switch and clicked it off. Outside the trees were lit faintly with moonlight reflected from the empty lake.

I sat down on the floor, out of the line of fire of anybody outside the window, and replaced the shell I had used with a new one in the chamber of my pistol. Then I called Sam, softly, and went outside, stopping to lock the door as I left. Sam came with me, alert now, feeling better. The milk had helped him. I put him in his pen and gave him a single word of command, "Keep."

Then I went down beside the dock at the end of my yard and took up the Fiberglas canoe that lay there. The paddle was under it. I carried it out to the water and launched it, making no sound.

Once again I wasn't going by the book. But the book wasn't written for one-man departments in the bush. The book was for guys with men to spare, able to lift the phone and call in the kind of support we used to get for a big push in Nam. I didn't have that kind of clout. If I lifted the phone and called the OPP for reinforcements, the best I could hope for would be a couple of cars full of bored officers with sirens wailing. They'd scare my birds away before I could close in on them. No. It had to be done this way, one man, kneeling in a canoe, paddling silently down to the marina.

I knew that's where they would be.

The *Mary Sue*, a cruiser, George had called it, sleeps six. He meant something big. She probably drew four feet of water. That meant she couldn't make it any closer to my place than the marina to tie up. And that meant that if the hoods had any mind for tactics, they would be tied up at the very end of the dock, giving them room to cut and run in one swoop once the first heavy-footed copper came down the length of the dock. On top of which they would have a well-lighted target for about twenty-five yards. There was nowhere for a man on the dock to hide.

I was hoping they would be expecting their own man. The classic way to handle their situation would be to wait at the end of the dock until their man came trotting back from my place with the envelope under his arm. With luck, that's all they would look out for. They wouldn't watch the channel. And that's the way I planned to reach them.

The water was still. A loon was laughing its idiot laugh away up the lake behind me, frogs were planging away in the weeds at the water's edge, and my canoe was making a tiny singing sound as the paddles made a tiny froth of the wake. I had to force myself to keep breathing. My heart was tense in my chest. I paddled wide of the dock, moving silently, then I turned and came in toward the bow, three-quarters on. It figured there would be no man there. The bow was narrow with no room to sit. If they had a man posted he would be at the stern, in the shadow of the upper deck, watching the only way he expected trouble to come, down the dock.

I inched the canoe through the water. I knew they wouldn't waste any time if they saw a copper coming at them. The best I could hope for was that they would try to run me down in the cruiser. More likely they would level up their pistols and blow holes in me as I got in range. But I couldn't hurry. I had to arrive at the boat with no forward motion to jar them when I touched. One shock and they would be all over me.

Slowly I made my way alongside, turning the canoe so it slid alongside the hull, bringing me under a lighted window.

I braced my fingertips against the hull, inching myself upright. It was like moving on skates for the very first time. An inch too much movement, an ounce too much pressure and my feet would have slid out from under me, leaving me doing fish impressions while the heavies whaled away at me with their artillery.

I managed it. I moved so slowly my flesh felt like it would creep right off my bones. I had aged a year by the time my fingers found the deck level and I could pull myself up straight. The drapes were drawn almost across. I could see through a wedge-shaped slot that made everything inside a jigsaw puzzle with most of the pieces missing.

There was a long tan shape, lower than my eyes. And there was a truncated slab of blue with dark brown below it. And there was white. Two tones of white. Flesh and white nylon.

I stared at it, drawing the missing pieces in with my mind. Then the blue slab moved and I could see it was a man's arm in a short-sleeved shirt. And I could see the white. It was Angela Masters's side. And her brassiere.

It looked as if the boys had forgotten business for a while. Slowly I inched the canoe along the hull until I was level with the dip at the back of the deck. Nobody was there. Whoever should have been on sentry duty was someplace else. Maybe up on the land end of the dock, waiting for the dead guy to come back. Maybe inside, waiting for his turn with the prisoner.

Slowly and deliberately I put my full weight on the edge of the deck. If the boat dipped, nobody felt it but me. Then I shoved the canoe away from me with my foot and squirmed on deck, under the safety line. Moving slowly was agony. Any moment a man could come out of the cabin and jump on my hands and pin me. No clever unarmed combat trick can get you out of that situation. You don't get into it. Period. Unless you're a dumb, single-handed copper, trying to earn his day's

145

pay. When I was all aboard, I rose to my knees, watching out over the side of the hull, toward the end of the dock as I drew my gun.

Ahead of me three steps led down to the covered area around the door of the cabin. I went down them, a millimeter at a time, straining my ears to hear what was going on. The only sound was a faint mewing as if somebody was playing too roughly with a kitten. I covered my gun with my left hand while I cocked it, muffling the little click. Then I straightened up, slammed the door open, and stepped inside, crouching low and to the right.

"Hold it," I said.

Blue Shirt looked around as if his mother had caught him playing with the little girl next door. He was big and blank faced, his chin almost as blue as his shirt with five-o'clock shadow. Angela Masters was sitting in a chair. She was tied there. Her mouth was gagged with a towel. Her brassiere was pulled up over her breasts. Her eyes were wide with ten kinds of emotion. For a moment I wanted to pull the trigger. Instead I told Blue Shirt, "Face down. On the floor."

God. I was slow. So slow. I should have done what was needed. I should have put a hole through the far door in the saloon. I would have, but I'm not a soldier anymore. Just a policeman.

Blue Shirt looked at me, rolling the whites of his eyes, and sank to his knees as if I were an idol.

And then, in the first moment that had tasted like victory since the case began, the voice spoke from the crack in the far door. "I've got a gun on the broad, copper. Drop the gun."

I still could have fired. In that echoing eternity before the voice died away I could have put two shots through the door, hoping that one of them at least would hit the other man, take his mind off murder.

But I didn't. I am not a killer. The girl might die. Maybe I might, but that was old news. The girl was a stranger to death. As a peace officer, I had to see she stayed that way.

The door opened a crack more and I could see the gun barrel trained on the girl's back. It was a big gun. A Magnum. It would pulp her, flinging her torn meat around the cabin like dishrags. And then Blue Shirt was getting up off his knees again, careful not to come between me and the doorway. He was grinning, a big stupid grin that showed teeth with a lot of gold in them.

"Keep to one side and take his gun," the voice said. Blue Shirt came closer, still not sure. And then the voice told me, "Put it on the floor, facing you."

There was only one emotion in the girl's eyes now. If it had words to it, it would have been a prayer.

Slowly I did as I was told.

The door opened then and the other guy came out. He was dark and slick, his hair swept up on his head and lacquered in place, as shiny and metallic as the .357 he held in his left hand. He beamed. He had done his trick.

I kept my face blank. It wouldn't help to let him know that his skin was cruddy and he stank of cologne and that I could see no need for him in the cosmic scheme of things.

Blue Shirt pounced on my gun, grabbed it as if it were hot, and sprang back, pointing it at me. He looked so happy I thought the other guy was going to pat him on the head and tell him "good boy."

The other guy didn't. He said to me, "So you're the big tough guy, are you?"

There was no answer. I made none.

The other guy was slinging my gun from hand to hand like Billy the Kid. He cackled with laughter. "Hey. I'm a cop, Joey. How 'bout that."

Brooklyn, I thought. And waited while the .357 pointed at me. I memorized every line of the face, every detail of the clothing. He was perhaps fifty. A little round in the waist. Wearing an expensive monogrammed sport shirt and pale green slacks held up with an alligator belt.

He came up to me and slapped me across the face. "Gonna remember me, are you? Maybe this'll help," he said, and slapped me again. I pursed my lips to save my teeth and waited. He did it a couple of times more, breaking the skin with his fancy diamond ring. Then he changed tactics and swung at me with the gun barrel. I hit him hard, up under the armpit, close to the heart. He went ooomph and for a moment it felt good. Then the other guy, Blue Shirt, was leveling my own gun at my chest and I knew it was no use.

Fancy Shirt straightened up, the gun still in his left hand but hanging low as he stared at me with a hatred more intense than anything I had ever seen before. Slowly he raised the gun level with my chest and I thought it was over. Instead he spoke to his workhorse. "Kick him," he said.

I've been worked over before. But this bastard was an expert. I managed to save my face and my testicles. One kick in either spot and it was their game. And I fell and rolled under the table where he couldn't get a clear swing at me. But he hurt me. He hurt me a lot.

Finally his master's voice said "okay" and he stopped, as neatly responsive as Sam might have been.

I lay there, waiting for the next move. My mind was working at enormous speed. I knew that they would not shoot. Not now, now I was cornered. They didn't want the neighboring people to hear. I was safe. Until they took this rig out of the dock and up to mid-channel. Then any fighting I had to do would be for the big money.

Fancy Shirt said, "You gonna remember me now, huh?"

I nodded. Obedient now. We'd worry about later when it happened. He took out a pack of Winstons and shook it until one came loose. He lifted it out with his lips, the way they do in movies. His eyes were on me all the time and the creepy

148

movement of his mouth had a sneering, sexual challenge to it.

Blue Shirt kept me covered with my gun while he found a lighter and lit up for his boss. Then the elegant one laid the Magnum on the table. "You got something belongs to her," he said. "Her" came out "hor." Another New Yorker. Another heavy.

I said, "What do you mean?"

He sighed, picked up his gun again, and nodded to Blue Shirt, who landed three quick kicks on the same part of my shin. My eyes watered up with pain.

" 'kay," the boss said, and the kicking stopped.

"You got a 'n envelope she gave you," he explained.

This time I nodded. "Right."

My eyes were clearing. I was able to see that his nails were neat, manicured.

"Yeah. Well, she shoulda given it to me, y'unnerstan?"

"You must want it pretty bad," I said.

"Bad enough to keep kickin' you till we get it," he told me.

"I used to play football," I said, and braced myself for the quick flurry of pain.

The boss said, "Shee-it. We got ourselves a goddamn hero." The kicking stopped.

"Maybe we're kickin' the wrong one," he said. "Unless you can think of some other games to play with her."

I looked at the girl. Her eyes were closed but tears were running down her cheeks. Her face had withered. She knew what they could do, without pleasure or remorse, to get what they wanted.

Blue Shirt stuffed my gun into his belt. I hoped for a moment that it was still cocked, that it might go off and give me back a two-second opportunity. But he had closed the hammer. It was safe, a lump of lifeless metal. Now he took a knife out of his pocket and flicked it open.

149

He went over to the girl and grabbed one breast. As he turned to his boss for the command I gave in.

"Okay. I'll give it to you." I could taste my own bile. I knew now who had cut Winslow's throat. I could imagine his grinning face as the old man gurgled and died.

"Where is it?" Fancy Shirt asked me.

"I hid it, in my yard. I'll take you there."

Angela Masters had opened her eyes again and was looking at me. I did not care what her eyes were trying to say.

"Smart," the boss said. He flicked his head to the other guy. "Get some rope, tie his hands up good," he said.

I said nothing. If I was lucky they would not use my handcuffs. Rope was bad, but cuffs would put me out of the race for keeps. Blue Shirt found some rope and came back. I turned on my face like a good little boy while he knelt on my spine and lashed my hands together. By opening my hands wide and flat I was able to stop him from tightening the rope completely, but he was strong and I felt my pulses throb as the blood started my hands swelling helplessly.

The boss got impatient at last. "Awright awready," he said. The guy got off my back. I lay there, looking at the broadloom and at Angela Masters's feet. The boss said, "You stay here, keep the broad quiet. No fooling around, huh? Keep an eye out for Freddie. An' for the local guy." Blue Shirt hoisted me to my feet, levering me up by the wrists. I came up, it was impossible not to, but I was starting to hope. If only one of them went with me, I had a chance. I had Sam.

As I stood there, waiting, I saw the tan shape that I had glimpsed through the window. It was Pardoe, stretched out on a bunk, rolled against the wall blankly, like a bundle of laundry. His breath was ugly, snoring. He had a concussion. The boss considered this. "If the Limey wakes up, don't do nothing. Just keep him quiet, awright?"

The kicker said, "Yuh."

150

The boss man took hold of my hair. He had to reach up quite a way to do it. "Let's go," he said.

I went. My chance was coming.

He pushed me up the stairs and to the side. He balanced me, by my hair, as I stepped over the rail and down on to the dock. He walked me along the dock, keeping behind me, his hands off my hair. Anyone looking out of the port of a cruiser would have thought we were two friends taking a stroll. I checked all around as I walked. He had mentioned a local man. I wanted to see him if I could. But there was nobody there. At the end of the dock cars were lined up. He took me to one of them, a late model Caprice. I couldn't see the license. He unlocked it, then undid the rear door and threw me in, across the seat. "Stay on your face and pull your legs in," he said. I obeyed. My hands were pulsing so hard I was worried about being able to use them again that night, if I got the chance. He sat in the front and started the motor quietly. Then he drove off, moving just as quietly, a discreet, careful tourist not wanting to disturb the other revelers. Nice guy.

He drove to my place and stopped, under the Manitoba maple out front. I started to worry about the dead man inside. If Fancy Shirt found the body, I was a dead man too. They would get the envelope first. There's a limit to the pain anyone can stand. After that I would be face down in the lake, what was left of me. I remembered Blue Shirt and his knife and shuddered. As we got out of the car, Sam barked. I recognized his duty sound, an ugly snarling roar that would keep anybody away from him and the envelope.

The driver got out. He stood for a second or two and called "Freddie?" in a soft, inquiring way. The only reply was Sam's bark. The man swore once and opened the back door of the car. My feet folded down and I wiggled backward and stood up. He grabbed my wrists and twisted. I bit down on the pain and came with him. "Where is it?" he asked.

151

I said, "Turn the lights off or the dog will keep on barking."
He leaned into the car and switched off the lights. He was
carrying the gun in his right hand now.

"Where is it?" he asked again.

"In the dog pen," I told him and he swore.

"You think I'm gonna believe that?"

"Where would you have hid it?" I asked.

He swore and said, "Let's go."

We walked down to Sam's cage, me in front. Sam was
patroling and barking, the way I had trained him over long
slow months. "Shut him up," the man said and I told Sam
"easy." That was the cue word, warning him to wait for the
next command. He stopped barking and stood still, a handsome silent show dog, not a threat.

The man had gone to the house and was trying the door. It
was locked. He rattled it a couple of times, then came back to
join me. I thanked my good fairy that the dead man's wild
bullet hadn't come through the door or the window. It just
looked as if he had gone. Fancy Shirt prodded me with the
gun. "Get the envelope."

"You'll have to open the door for me," I said.

"Cute," he sneered. "Then what?"

"Then I go in and get the envelope. Unless you want to."

"You get it," he said. "And don't screw around or you're
dead."

"Don't do that." I sounded pitiful. I didn't want him tenser
than he had to be.

Slowly and carefully he slid the bolt back, keeping his gun
trained on Sam now. He was scared. I could tell by the way he
kept even the tips of his fingers clear of the wire. The animal
in his own little soul respected Sam's ferocity. He was still
enough in control not to pull the trigger on Sam. He didn't
want to risk that cannon of his waking up the few people who

lived within a hundred yards of here. He had that much control, but that was all.

"Don't get cute," he told me. His voice had the rasp of fear in it.

"I won't," I said. "I don't want any more trouble."

He pulled gently on the door, keeping it between himself and the eighty-pound menace of my last trump card. The door was made the same way as the rest of the pen, chain-link fencing over iron pipes. It was on good metal hinges that moved easily. He nudged me in the back of the leg with his foot. "Move," he said. I went into the pen. Sam dropped and fawned in front of me, whining gently. He knew I was in trouble and wanted to help, but his training was keeping him back. I'd told him "easy." I bumped him with my knee. "Easy," I told him again and he straightened up.

My voice was level, the tone I used for commands. He realized it and came to my heel, licking my swollen fingers. "Easy," I told him again and he stopped licking and walked behind me as I went slowly for his dish. When I reached it I knelt down and picked it up, twisting my body sideways to reach it. I turned it over in my clumsy fingers, feeling the envelope that was still taped underneath it.

The man at the gate was anxious. He had lit a cigarette. The glow of the red point made a mask of his features. He called out, "Come on. What's keepin' you."

I turned away from him, pretending to fumble with the dish while my head came down close to Sam's ears. "Come!" I whispered, and saw him stiffen at the command. Holding the dish behind me I came back to the gate.

Fancy Shirt was holding it shut, his foot wedged against the bottom of it. He was puffing his cigarette fiercely, like some exercise his doctor had told him to keep up. "Slip it underneath," he commanded.

"I can't. It's taped to the bottom of the dog dish."

He swore. "Come here," he said.

I went to the door, Sam a few inches behind me and to my left. He was in the classic "heel" position, ready for the next command.

The man opened the door about four inches. "Turn around and hand it to me," he said.

I turned, preparing myself for the next moment. The man had to handle his gun and the bowl and keep the gate almost closed. He would probably poke the gun barrel through the wire of the gate as far as the fore sight. That was the way I would have done it. I put out of my mind what would happen if the fore sight jammed in the wire. My spine would be only inches away from the muzzle when he fired.

I felt for the edge of the gate with my fingers, and I spoke to him, starting in a soothing tone. As the gate came to my hand I said, "What's up, you think we'd be fool enough to *fight?*" I roared the last word as a command to Sam, yanking the door open as I did so.

Sam passed me in mid-air, leaping for the man's gun hand. I swung around on one foot, poised for the kick that would win or lose the day.

The gun roared and Sam fell out of the air. And at the same instant my foot caught the gun man squarely in the testicles.

He groaned and dropped his hand, crouching over while I swung the second kick that snapped his jaw like a dead stick. He flew backward. He might have been trying to fire—I didn't stop to check. I jumped, both feet on his abdomen.

His breath came out of him and he lay still.

I knelt down, peering into his face for any sign of a counterattack. I would have smashed his face again with my forehead. But there was no need. The eyes were open, but he was out cold, the face foreshortened with the injury to the jaw.

I crouched and listened for any breathing. There was none.

I straightened up, aware that my shirt was sticky with Sam's blood. I stood up and went over to look at the ruin of my dog. And I could have wept for joy. He was alive. The bullet had ripped half his ear away. It was bleeding fast, and Sam was whimpering with pain. But he would make it.

I found the man's gun and kicked it in front of me over to the garage. The door at the side was unlocked and I went in and rummaged in the drawer until I came up with a hacksaw. Working with numb fingers I managed to set it into the vise and crank it up. After that it took only a moment to get free.

I spent a minute rubbing the circulation back into my hands. Then I checked the gun. It was too big for my police holster, so I stuck it in my belt. Then I went back to the man I had beaten. Looking down at him now with two free hands and a gun, it was hard not to think I had gone too far, been too rough. But it had been him or me. His breath had returned. It was ragged and clumsy, but it had the beginnings of a pattern to it. As I looked closely at him his lips began to move. I leaned down close to listen and heard him whisper all the bad language he had ever heard. Then I took out my cuffs and snapped his left wrist to a bar of Sam's cage.

I left him and went into the house. I had to brace myself against the cold fear of entering the room where the dead mobster lay. But I did it. And I dialed the station number. George Horn answered on the second ring. "Murphy's Harbour P'lice." I felt overcome with relief at his voice. Thank god for steady people, good people who would stay where you put them and do the job you gave them. I said "Hello, George . . ." and the kid was all over me.

"Hi, Reid. That Mr. Fullwell just rang. He says that it's important you get the message."

"What message?"

"About Straiton Chemical." He stumbled over the name in

155

his rush. "He says they're sharing time on the computer with some outfit called Datistics. It's a new company and the guy who runs it did time once for fraud. He says that's likely where the information came from." He paused, uncertain. "Does that make any sense to you?"

"Yeah," I said. "It makes the most sense of anything I've heard since this whole thing started." I paused for a moment, getting my thoughts back in a straight line.

George cut into the silence. "Hey, Reid. You okay?"

"Yeah. But I got a lot of jobs for you. A lot's been happening."

"Shoot," he said and I shook my head at the craziness of the word.

"One guy's been shot," I said. "And another guy needs a hospital. And Sam is hurt bad."

George's voice lost ten years. He was a frightened kid again. "Somebody hurt Sam?"

"Yeah. He got shot too. I think he'll make it, but he's bleeding pretty bad. If you can round up a vet, send him over to my yard, but don't do it first."

"What's first?" he asked in a low voice.

"First off. Call the OPP. Tell them to bring riot gear, tear gas, shotguns, the whole disaster. I want them at the marina. Next, order up a doctor and ambulance for the marina. There's a guy there with a bad head injury. But warn them not to move in until they get the word. You got that?"

"Right." He rattled the details back at me, and I went on. "After that, send an ambulance to the back of my place, there's a sick citizen cuffed to Sam's pen. And get the OPP homicide squad because there's a heavy in my kitchen with a hole in him."

His voice was an awed whisper that rasped on me like sandpaper, reminding me who I was and what I did best. "Jesus Christ, Reid. I ain't never met nobody like you."

156

I didn't comment. "Vet, OPP to the marina, ambulances, homicide. Okay?"

"Yeah," he said. "Ten-four."

I stepped around the dead man on the floor and opened the kitchen cupboard. I keep paper towels in there and I tore off a couple of yards from the roll. Then I opened a drawer and pulled out some clothespins I'd found when I rented the place. I'd never used them before, but tonight they might save Sam's life.

I went out to Sam and pressed some of the towels over the torn ear. Blood was pulsing out and it soaked the paper in seconds, but I knew it would stop if I could apply pressure. I pegged the paper to his ear with the clothespins, three of them close together. They would pinch in and help stop the blood. Sam whimpered once and made to scratch at his ear. I guessed he was still deaf from the explosion and shock, but I raised one finger to him and he lay still. Then I patted him once and went to the hood's car.

I was afraid someone might have heard the gunshot, but no lights were showing anywhere. Everyone was too drunk or scared or uninterested to wonder about things that go bump in the night. And if the man on the boat had heard he would probably have just grinned and figured it was his boss finishing me off.

The car keys were in the ignition. I started it up and pulled on the headlights. The handcuffed man on the grass made a feeble gesture in the light. It could have been an appeal for help. I backed up and drove away. He would live.

I thought as I drove. If Blue Shirt was still on his own, I could take him. He was stupid. He would probably try to use the girl as a hostage if it came to a showdown. He had seen that work once. If I was quick enough, he wouldn't get the chance to think that deeply.

There was a tinge of gray in the blackness of predawn as I

reached the marina. It would be light in half an hour and all the rules would change again. For now, I had cover.

I stopped the car at the very end of the dock and came out of it on the run. I heard the starter whining as I ran. The fool hadn't thought to start up ahead of time. I could make it. Without hesitation I drew the huge Magnum I'd taken off the guy at my place and fired twice, low down, right at the waterline where the slugs would smash the motor. I heard the starter motor stop with an agonized screech of metal. And then cursing, high and fluent.

I crouched low beside the boat and shouted. "Police. You're surrounded. Come out with your hands up."

The same voice went on cursing. Then there was a quick scream from Angela Masters and silence.

I waited for thirty seconds, hearing a heavy blundering sound as someone clumsy moved around in the cabin. It was my friend with the kicking shoes, tripping over his feet in the dark. Then the swearing voice spoke. Still high and frightened, but talking very slowly. "Hey, copper. You hear me?"

I crouched low. He might be testing me out, waiting to draw a bead on my voice and put a bullet out through the hull of the boat. I could die, but I could not shoot back. Not with two civilians in there with him.

I reached out with the muzzle of the pistol and tapped on the hull, arm's length from my body. "Yeah," I said. "I hear you." No bullet came through the hull. Instead I heard the girl whimper. He was using her as a shield. He could kill her. When he spoke again, his voice was breathless. The girl was struggling. Maybe other men at other times might think her willowy. He was finding her all sinew.

He said, "I got the broad."

I waited and he shrieked, "Okay?"

"Okay," I said.

"So me and her is comin' out. Try and stop me and she's dead. Unnerstan?"

158

"Then what?" I kept my voice irritated. He was expecting obedience; I had to rattle him.

"You keep outta my way," he shouted. "I'll kill her. I killed people before."

"Big shot. So you kill the broad. Then I plug you." I had to get him angry at me.

He bit. "Just don't try nothin' smart, copper."

Slowly as sunrise, I stood up and paced backward from the boat. Then, standing in the center of the dock, about twelve paces off I threw down my heavy lignum vitae night stick. It clattered like metal on the wooden dock. "You win," I called out. "Come on, I just threw down my gun." I watched without moving as the big man came up out of the shadows. My right hand was behind my back, holding the cocked Magnum. His head rose above the black outline of the deck. Then the girl's head came in sight, only an inch or two below his. I stood and waited, suspended in timelessness while the pair of them came right up on to the deck, their faces white in the blue clarity of the sodium light over the marina.

I watched for his gun. If he was clever, it would be pointed at the girl's head. It wasn't. He was too primitive for such cunning. It was out to one side, pointing vaguely at me. Unless the guy was the Lone Ranger, I was safe.

Now it all depended on the girl.

I started talking, to him but *at* the girl. "Okay. So you're out on deck and I don't have a gun. What're you waiting for? Why don't you *jump?*"

The girl beat me to it by a half second. She slid neatly down from under his arm and sprang forward over the rail.

In the same instant the big man snapped off a shot at me, and I fired.

The bullet hit him high in the chest on the right side. His arm with my police gun in it flew back over his head in a lazy arc that flung the gun into the water. And he flopped and rolled backward into the deck well, slithering down the steps

159

with a dead uselessness. I came up on him at a run. It was unnecessary. He was smashed up. The hydrostatic shock had probably killed him outright. The girl was sitting on the dock, leaning back against the boat, sobbing.

I stood for a moment, looking down on her blond head and thin white shoulders, naked except for the frivolity of her brassiere. The world was coming back to its proper pace. The killing had ended and the paperwork was about to begin. I gave myself a moment to step over the bleeding man and go down into the cabin of the cruiser. There was a nylon shell hanging on a hook inside the door. I took it and went back out, climbing down wearily from the boat to the dock.

"Here. Put this on," I told her.

She was still sobbing. I crouched to comfort her. "Don't cry anymore. You're all right now. It's all over." It should have been. People should have been scrambling out of their beds in the boats tied up farther back down the dock or in the rented rooms at the lakeshore tavern. But if they were, it wasn't quick enough to help me.

Cold metal jolted against the nape of my neck, nudging me and pulling back. And a voice behind me said, "Oh no, it isn't over."

I turned my head, very slowly, knowing the cold metal was the barrel of a gun.

It was a shotgun, held by a tall figure that I stared at for a long moment before I spoke.

"Okay, Murph. What's the game?"

Murphy said, "No game, Reid. Just drop your gun."

I didn't move fast enough for him and he jabbed me with the shotgun. I laid the big pistol on the dock. He scuffed it over the side with his toe. It plopped quietly into the water.

"Now what?" I asked him.

He waved the gun barrel in a tiny circle. He was a yard from me, too far for me to make a grab for the barrel, too close to miss if he pulled the trigger. He told me, "I haven't killed anybody since the war, but I haven't forgot how."

I said nothing and he sniffed impatiently. "Where's the envelope?" I tapped my shirt front.

"Right here where it would get holes in it if you pull that trigger."

He rocked on his metal leg and laughed. "I'll just have to blow your goddamn feet off then, won't I? That'll make you do like I say."

The girl was putting the shell on, sobbing intermittently like a child who is better now but doesn't want you to think so. She said, "What's happening? Why are you pointing the gun?"

Murphy ignored her. "Gimme the envelope, that's what I want," he told me.

Slowly I pulled it out of my shirt front and dropped it in front of him on the deck. He kept me covered tight as he crouched and picked it up.

I didn't speak or move as he tore it open at the corner with his teeth. He felt inside it with the tip of his finger. I saw him smile, a slow creasing of his face in the thickening dawn light. "How much good do you think that's gonna do you? All it will get you is two bits' worth of lead from these bastards," I said.

He said, "Shut up. We're takin' a boat ride."

The girl whimpered. "Where to? What's happening?"

He backed away up the dock. I glanced at the cruisers. Nobody was moving. Maybe they would talk about us later in the day. When our bodies were found and our pictures were put in the paper. For now, we were alone.

"Do as he says," I told the girl.

She came with me, following as Murphy backed up the dock until he came to a small cedar strip, like the police boat.

"Get in by the motor," he told me. I did. "You in the middle," he told the girl. She looked at me, her face clear now as dawn came up on us, gray and treacherous but with enough light to see by. I nodded at her. She stepped in and sat down.

Murphy stooped and pulled the bowline clear. He had it tied with a highwayman's hitch, so it pulled clear one-handed. "Start the motor," he said, stepping down into the bow seat. I fiddled with the choke, but he snapped at me, "Don't play games. Half an inch of choke and pull hard, out of gear."

I did as he said. The motor burbled and started. I pushed the choke back in and turned to face him. He waved me to back out, away from the dock. I let go the stern line and put the boat into reverse. Then I turned it and headed out into the channel. "Up the main channel," he commanded. Then he patted the gun with his claw of a bad hand. "And don't forget what's pointing at you." I moved out into mid-channel and opened the motor up. It was no good arguing with him. A shotgun from five feet away will take you in half. The girl kept looking at me. I ignored her. It was cold on the water and I began to shiver, envying Murphy his old plaid jacket. Somehow the cold was more immediate than the danger.

By the time we had gone through the narrows I knew where we were headed. It was the reference point I had seen on Winslow's map. I kept in mid-channel, remembering the spot from the description I had drawn myself when I saw the cross in pencil, yesterday. We were just about there when Murphy gestured with the gun. "Stop here."

I stopped, slamming the throttle shut in case it might throw Murphy off balance. It didn't. He rocked and stabilized, like a gyroscope. It was thudding silent with the motor stopped. Dawn was all around us now. Birds were calling. Mist was drifting over the surface of the water. It was all very goddamn romantic, except for Murphy and his gun. "What's going on?" I made it sound bored, but I wanted to know. I had to know if we were going to survive.

"I'm waiting for a pickup," Murphy said with a dry half-chuckle. "Very modern, Reid. Just like Viet Nam. I've got air support."

162

"Somebody's coming to get that envelope?"

"By float plane," he said. "Smart, eh? No need to file a flight plan. Those guys skip over the border and back with no problems at all. Just set down on a lake and take what they want."

"And they want this envelope. Why?"

"I don't know why. I just know this is big." He was like a kid at the movies. He was just waiting for the nice men to buy him a box of popcorn because he'd been a good boy.

"Did Winslow get you into this?" I was talking past the girl, who was swinging her head from one of us to the other, too frightened to talk. A lot had happened to her over the last twenty-four hours, probably including rape. She was saturated with horrors. All she wanted was for it to be over.

Murphy jutted his good leg up and rested the barrel of the shotgun on top of it. I recognized the gun now in the light. It was the pump gun from the office.

"Yeah," he said. "Ross asked me for some help. I helped him before a time or two. Once they sent me a case of rye." Chickenshit payola. My mind was screaming but I needed more facts, more help before I could act.

"So what was the scam this time?"

"This time it was that a couple of guys was coming up to see somebody. They would need a boat to get there. And they would be carrying an envelope that Ross's friends wanted."

"So he stationed himself at the marina and acted dumb till they got there?"

"Right."

"And then he pulled that antique pistol of his on them, only Murray went for his gun and Ross slugged him."

"I guess that's how it was," Murphy said. "I never got a chance to talk to him after."

"Did you stop to think why not?" I yelled it. If I could break him down here and now it would save us from more risks.

163

"Because he goofed up." Murphy spat it out. "His first ever chance at the big time and he messed it up."

Suddenly Angela Masters spoke. She was angry and proud. "Yes, he was beaten by a better mind," she said.

"Pardoe?" I prodded.

"Yes." Her face puckered up into something like triumph. "He found out they weren't taking him where he wanted to go, so he cut the lines with his pocketknife. And then he jumped overboard and swam for shore and came back to the hotel."

It all made sense now. The empty boat had been abandoned when Winslow had followed Pardoe over the side in a desperate bid to keep him. Only Pardoe must have swum farther, faster and Winslow had gone ashore to the closest land, the island, where he had stolen my boat. It all made sense, all of it, except the motive.

We heard the sound of an aircraft. Low and close, coming over the trees in a shallow run, just about on a straight line for us.

"Start the motor and keep it in neutral," Murphy told me.

"Why? So you can hand over the disk?" I laughed. "What do you think I'm gonna do when we get ashore?"

"You're not getting ashore," he said evenly. "I'm going on the plane. You and her are going to have a little suicide pact." The plane was in sight. It would be with us in another minute.

"It won't wash," I told him. "Your fingerprints are all over the gun."

"And so are yours," he said. "This is the office gun. You loaded it yourself yesterday morning."

I thought the girl was going to faint. But I turned away and started the motor. We had a good chance to win. We were going to win, unless all my luck had gone.

I put the boat in reverse and backed gently out of the line in which the plane was approaching. Murphy watched me carefully, saying nothing. He was counting the money he would have in a few moments. He was going to be rich, to make up for all the years of being nobody in the town named for his family. He thought. The plane came down, a high-wing monoplane on floats. A Cessna 119, I thought. It landed where we had been sitting.

The door opened. A face peeped out.

"Take it over there, nice and slow," Murphy said.

"No chance," I told him. I slammed the engine into forward and sprang ahead with all the force the boat could muster. The pilot would have no chance. All I had to worry about was Murphy. He shouted for me to stop, and then I saw the end of the gun as he lifted and aimed it at my head. My flesh clenched hopelessly on my bones as he pulled the trigger. And nothing happened. He pumped the action and fired again. Nothing. And nothing again. And then we hit the plane, crunching one of the floats so the wingtip dipped into the drink.

The impact flung Murphy back almost over the side of the boat. I pulled him in and slapped him hard across the mouth. Then I backed up, keeping dead astern of the plane where the shouting of the crew was filling the air with a fury that was going to turn into bullets in a second or two more.

I turned and pulled away. Behind us the pistols banged and flapped like Chinese firecrackers. I found myself hooting with laughter, unable to contain myself. I had won. I had won, single bloody handed.

I was still laughing when we got back to the dock and I handed Murphy over to the OPP.

13

$\mathbf{I}$t took a month for the news to get out of the papers. First I was a hero. Then Sam was a hero. Then we were rotten killers. I had the same dizzy sense of déjà vu that had taken over when it happened before in the city.

Only this little town didn't let me down.

I guess they're rednecked enough to appreciate the use of necessary force; in fact, they tried to get me a decoration for valor. The police commission wouldn't go along with it, but I kept my job. And Sam lived. He lay on the floor at my feet one late afternoon in Indian summer while I caught up on the everyday stuff.

I was thinking about closing up and trying for pickerel down at the lock, using a new horsehair jig that George had made for me, when the door opened and Fullwell came in. He looked spry. New suit, even a new hat. He was celebrating the raise they gave him for his part in sorting out the case, and writing up Murray as a hero. Security companies like that kind of publicity. It gets them customers, sometimes even lets them put their rates up.

Fullwell took off his new hat and shook hands with me. We

did all the buddy-buddy things of asking one another how it's going. Then I cracked out the office bottle and we sat and sipped rye out of coffee mugs.

"You know, there's one question nobody asked you," he admitted after a while, "and I'm still wondering how it came off." He sipped his booze and lowered the cup. "How come the shotgun wasn't loaded?"

I stood up and went over to the rack and patted the butt of the gun. "I unloaded it myself."

He frowned, scrunching his face up. "Why? Did you know ahead of time that Murphy was in on the deal, that you couldn't trust him?"

"Yeah." I sat down again and took another sip of my own drink. "Yeah. I knew as soon as the office had been raided. When I rang him, he didn't seem surprised. All he asked was, 'Did they get it?' Fullwell cranked up his frown an inch tighter. "Hell. He had no way of knowing whether it was some kids trashing the place or what. But he acted like it was the guys looking for the envelope. So I figured he was in on the deal. And I knew he didn't have a gun of his own, so I thought he might use one of the office guns if it came to a showdown."

"And you unloaded them." Fullwell grinned. He sipped his rye, shaking his head in disbelief at my smartness. "Another thing," I added. "I got my confirmation when I found that slip in the pocket of the guy in my house. It was their alibi. Murphy must have given it to them some time after the killing. It made it look as if they'd been out of the lake when the killing happened."

Fullwell sipped, talking around his coffee cup. "Not just a pretty face, are you?"

I laughed and he went on, lowering his cup. "Hey, something else that's been bothering me, what happened to that diskette? It wasn't even mentioned at the trial."

"It was gone by then," I explained. "When we were coming

back in from wrecking that float plane I took the diskette from Murphy and gave it to the Masters girl. She threw it over the side."

She had told me what was on it, later. We became friendly during the trial. She was there as a witness. So was Pardoe, with his wife. He had come out of his coma loaded with guilt at leaving her. So Angela had been at loose ends. And I guess she figured she owed me. It turned out that the guys on the boat hadn't started on her when I got there. They'd been about to, just to pass the time. Blue Shirt was telling her how he liked it when I lumbered in. Fortunately for her he hadn't gotten past the advertising stage.

So we had a brief thing. And she told me about the diskette. Lying in my bed one morning with the light bouncing off the water onto my ceiling.

"Derek had isolated a way of synthesizing cocaine," she said. She was lying up on one elbow, stroking my chest, tracing the scar I have there from an argument I'd had that was settled with bayonets.

"I thought there was synthetic cocaine already, novocaine, stuff like that," I said.

She shook her head. "No. Those are derivatives. Cocaine has always been grown. And then Derek came across a way of cooking it as simply as you can cook up amphetamines."

"And the people at the computer time-sharing place realized what he was doing?"

She flopped down, laying her ear flat over the scar as if some message would come up out of that line of whitened hide and pass directly to her. I stroked her hair. "They knew what he was on to. And then when he got the answer and didn't feed it into the computer's memory, just put it on a diskette and kept it, they came after him."

"So he ran up here to find his boss. And the mob knew that Winslow was one of their boys, so they primed him to wait for

168

Pardoe and deliver him to them aboard a cruiser they'd hired."

She nodded, a comforting scrubbing motion of her hair over the roughness of my chest. "They really are organized in organized crime," she said.

I told Fullwell the clinical bits. He may have guessed about Angela, but he was too old a policeman to say anything. He just asked, "And she fired that diskette overboard, just like that?"

"Just like that. But I'm not looking to have a bunch of guys snorkeling up here looking for it, so treat it as confidential, okay?"

He shrugged, turning his head to let me know he felt the way I did. We drank in silence for a minute or so and then he asked, "And how about you and Sam. You gonna stay here?"

"It's a living." I bent down and tickled Sam's good ear. He squirmed pleasurably.

"How about the fink kid who sprayed 'Killer' on the side of the station?" Fullwell asked.

"I caught him," I said. "I made him an offer he couldn't refuse: paint the whole of the station the same color, or have Sam bite his ass out."

Fullwell laughed. "I saw the station was painted white. Now who painted 'Killer' on the side wall in black?"

"I'm working on that."

He got serious. It made him do a couple of stagy little things like actors do on TV. He took out his sunglasses and polished them with a Kleenex. Then he pulled a couple of faces and said, "We can give you work. Better work than this."

"I like this."

He made a fresh face. "It may not like you. People don't like policemen who kill people. You're a menace."

"So how do security companies feel?"

"About ten grand a year better. Pick your assignments."

I guess I looked surprised. He cranked up the pressure.

"No more dawn-to-dusk crap, regular holidays." He let it dangle like a frog with a hook through its lip, waiting for a smallmouth bass to take it.

I thought about it for a long time before speaking. "I'll let you know. I want to see a whole year come and go in this place. After that, it could get repetitious."

He drained his cup and put it down on the counter. "Well. The job will wait for you. But I can't. I'm on my way back to Toronto tonight."

We shook hands and he left and after a while I got up and went over to the shelf under the counter where I had put the jig George had made for me. It didn't look very convincing, just a tuft of black and white horsehair on a weighted hook. But then I'm not a pickerel.

Sam watched me as I opened my notebook and put it inside the cover for safety. I nodded to him. "Come on, fellah. Let's see if we're smarter than those walleyes."

He trotted after me and I went out of the door and headed for home to pick up my fishing rod. I was surprised to find I was whistling.